#1 All Isn't Well in ROSWELL!

written by K.B. Brege

illustrated by D. Brege

This book is a work of fiction. All names, characters, places and incidents are either products of the author's imagination, invented, or are used fictitiously. The aliens, however, might exist.

Proofreading: Linda Angér www.thewriteconcept.com

ISBN 0-9774119-0-7

Printed in USA

First Printing Paperback edition - November 2005

With love to our son who adds a sense of wonder and imagination to everyday. To our mothers who always encorage us to go for our dreams and provide love and support. To our sisters, gramps, and the troupe who help us live in the moment…and to all of those who believe.

Table of Contents

#1 All Isn't Well in ROSWELL!

Chapter One

"Miiiiccck! Mick, are you ready? We're leaving in five minutes!"

"I'll be right down, Mom! I just gotta find my flashlight! A-HA! There it is, under the bed!"

Hi! I'm Mick Morris, and welcome to my world. I know that this sounds like your everyday story – your mom yelling at you to hurry up, but my life is really very different. And when I say different, I'm not kidding!

Just to tell you a little bit about me, I'm 10 years old and in the fifth grade. I have straight brown hair and brown eyes; my mom says that they are the big, intense kind of eyes. I'm about average in height and size for a kid for my age. I usually wear blue jeans, but they have to be good jeans and a nice t-shirt. I just don't like the sloppy look. Don't get me wrong, I'm not picky, I just like to look nice. If I'm not traveling with my mom and dad, I'm inventing things or building robots. Those are my hobbies. I'm a pretty happy kid and I like to make people laugh.

I don't have any brothers or sisters, just a cat named Horace, two birds and some fish. I live in a regular house in the suburb of Oak Grove with my mom and dad.

We're close to the big city where my parents work, so we go there a lot. There are all kinds of cool things to do there, like museums, theaters, restaurants, and shops. And we almost always make a stop at the studio where my parent's show is filmed.

My parents have the ultimate job. They work for a cable station company called "Uncover." Their job is to produce a show called "Myth Solvers" for the station.

That's where I come in. I'm a Myth Solver. In case you aren't quite clear on what a myth is, I'll tell you. It's like a legend or a fable, one of those things that people aren't really quite sure if it happened in the past or if it is even happening now.

So we travel all over the world doing the Myth Solver show, trying to figure these things out. Sometimes we have to go to some pretty dark, scary places. That's why you are not going to believe some of the things that I am about to tell you. It will change the way you look at things forever.

Especially this trip – nobody could have convinced me in my wildest dreams that this type of thing could have ever happened to me. Well, that is, until it happened: *the scariest time of my life.*

Chapter Two

It was summer break. That is when we usually travel, on school breaks – Spring, Summer, and even on Winter break, to get footage for the shows.

Once my parents have filmed everything that they need from the locations, we head home. They continue to edit, which means putting the film together in the studio – and I go back to school.

We cover a lot of ground in the summers. On this particular trip, we were on our way to Roswell, New Mexico. I didn't think too much about it. What could really happen in a desert? Well let me tell you, *was I wrong!*

Roswell has a history of alien stories – UFO's (which stands for Unidentified Flying Objects), extra-terrestrials, and tales of alien life forms crashing to earth.

One of the most popular stories is about a rancher, who back in 1947 (yep, I'm talking years and years ago, before even our parents were born), had a mysterious thing happen on his property.

The rancher is said to have discovered some weird metal and wood that had crashed onto his ranch. He notified the local sheriff, who called in the Military - there's an Air Force base in Roswell known as Area 51. The Air Force told the newspapers that the metal was from a flying saucer that had crashed to earth.

But, then the very next day, they said it wasn't a spaceship at all. In fact, they claimed that it was just a weather balloon that had been launched into orbit, and then fell to Earth.

Other wild, scary stories started to circulate. Like the story that about 100 miles from the original site, the entire ship had crashed, and aliens were scattered across the ground with the pieces of the ship. Real aliens! *They said that they were tiny little gray-green men with huge heads and enormous black eyes! They even said that one of them was still alive!*

Rumors started to spread that the aliens were rushed back to the military base. A nurse from the base told everyone that they had operated on the aliens. Then the nurse suddenly disappeared, and nobody ever heard from her again. From then on, everyone that was involved was told by the military to never, ever discuss what they had seen. No trespassing signs were put up all around the base. It became a mystery, and a myth – an *unsolvable* myth in Roswell, New Mexico.

Crazy as it all sounds, some people say it really happened, and some say it was just a made-up story or a practical joke. Myth or reality, we were on our way to solve it. We were going to the actual site where the rancher had discovered the aliens almost 60 years ago. *Little did I know that I would discover a lot more than that!*

Chapter Three

"Miiick! C'mon! The RV is packed and ready to go! We've got a deadline to meet!" Dad yelled.

"OK, coming!" I answered.

I just needed one more thing – my book about Roswell and the story of the aliens. I knew that if we were heading to Roswell, I was going to have to do some research. I grabbed the book off my nightstand, threw it in my backpack, and ran downstairs.

"Ready to go?" Dad asked.

He was in a great mood, but then again he usually is. He's a big guy, tall with wide shoulders. He looks like a football player, and in fact, he did play football in college. He has the same brown hair as I do, but with bright blue eyes. He is a super funny guy, and loves to tease my mom.

My mom is a happy person too. She is short, with wavy blond hair. She loves our family and our home, which is why it's weird to me that she has a job traveling so much. She's also an awesome cook, and funny too.

Dad always says that she's full of sass. They really love to have fun. They always say, "What's the point – if you can't enjoy your life?" That has become our family motto.

"Yep, got everything I need," I replied, or so I thought. I had no idea that no matter how much I thought I was prepared for this trip, I could have never predicted what I'd be in for.

"Great! Mom's just getting the last few things from the fridge and we'll be on our way," Dad answered.

One of the cool things about traveling across the country was that we rode in this huge recreational vehicle, known as an RV for short. It looked like a giant bus. It's what rock stars and bands travel in, so it made me feel pretty cool.

On the outside it was painted shiny, metallic black with huge, green neon letters that said "Myth Solvers." It had swoops on it, an alien, and what looked like a Bigfoot footprint. It was like a house on wheels, with a bathroom, bedrooms, and a full kitchen – really sweet! We called it The Myth Mobile.

"OK, I think I have everything," Mom said.

"How about my sunflower seeds?" Dad asked.

"They're in there," Mom answered.

"Hey Mom, what about those awesome chips?" I asked.

"Got 'em," Mom replied.

We were ready to roll! I happily walked outside, ready to start loading my stuff into the Myth Mobile. But when I saw what I saw, I froze.

The site was unbearable. It…it was awful! No, worse than awful, it was horrible! My throat tightened and my stomach turned. I wanted to throw-up. It was more that I could handle. *I stopped dead in my tracks and just stared.*

Chapter Four

"Mick! Mick, watch out! I almost tripped over you!" Mom said as she briskly walked around me. "C'mon…we have to get moving here."

"Moooommm! Stop!" I said in a loud whisper. But it was too late. She was already standing next to…to…*IT!*

"Oh, didn't I tell you? Your cousin Sissy is coming with us," Mom replied, as she patted Sissy on the head.

"What? Sissy is coming with us?" I said, frustrated – forcing the fakest smile of my life.

"Yes, and so is your Uncle Hayden," Mom answered in her matter-of-fact voice – the voice that means she knows that I am about to freak out.

"Your Aunt Marisa is scheduled to work at the hospital all week, and Uncle Hayden is on vacation, so they're coming with us. Uncle Hayden is going to drive since Sam is on vacation, too." The instant mom turned and walked towards the Myth Mobile, Sissy turned on her heels, glared at me, and stuck out her tongue. *What a silly girl!*

I didn't care what Aunt Marisa and Uncle Hayden, or even Sam – a really cool older guy who was our regular driver – was up too. What I did care about was that we were going have to spend an entire week with the worst cousin in the whole wide world – *Sissy the Serpent!*

Sissy is her nickname, short for Cecilia. She acts like a spoiled brat, but never in front of grown-ups. That's when she fakes it, like she's the sweetest girl that you could ever meet. But when they aren't around, watch out! She is a tiny, snotty, persnickety girl who is no fun at all. All she ever cares about is that her short blonde hair always looks picture perfect, and that she never gets an ounce of dirt on her girlish pink outfits that always match exactly from head to toe. She even carries a pink backpack!

She hates everything fun – bugs, snakes, robots, slime, she doesn't even like video games! I walked toward the Myth Mobile, deciding that I was not going to let any stupid girl ruin my myth-solving mission. Then just like I thought, she did her usual hair fling and bounced my way.

"Hey Mick! Oh, can you just believe it? We're going to Roswell with you! I am soooo excited," Sissy chirped. "Do you think we will be able to go swimming?"

"Swimming?" I said as I glared at her with disgust. "*Swimming?* It's a desert, not an ocean! Besides, I have serious work to do there. Don't you know that people have claimed there have been actual alien landings and sightings in Roswell?"

"Aliens!" she laughed. "You can't be serious!"

"Apparently you know nothing about where we are going," I replied. "So I suggest that you read up on it before we get there."

I dug into my backpack and pulled out a book titled <u>The Roswell Truth and Other Aliens and Extraterrestrials in New Mexico</u>, and handed it to her.

"This is what you spend your time reading?" Sissy snipped.

"Yeah, and I suggest that you do too!" I replied, picking up my backpack.

"I don't believe in aliens! How foolish!" she said, tossing the book to the ground.

I sneered at her as I picked up my book, and then laughed. "Good! Then you won't have to worry about it when they abduct you!"

I never wanted to let her know that her bad behavior ever got to me.

But what I didn't know was that it didn't matter how much I read about aliens, or what I knew about Roswell and Area 51. It didn't even matter how badly Sissy behaved, or if she read the book and believed in aliens or not. *None of that mattered, because nothing could have prepared us for what was about to happen on this trip to Roswell, New Mexico.*

Chapter Five

I mapped out our route as the Myth Mobile rolled down the road. We had made it through seven states, already crossed the New Mexico border, and had just a short time left to go. Then I could escape into the desert on my myth-solving mission. Better yet, I could escape from Sissy the Serpent. I had all but had it by now, especially when she drank the last orange juice. That really frosted me.

Everyone was asleep except Uncle Hayden and me. I looked at my light-up watch. It was 11:00 p.m., and I was getting tired. Just as my eyes started to close, the Myth Mobile lunged violently!

Books, suitcases, and plates – everything went flying! Uncle Hayden swerved to the left, then to the right! My mother and Sissy screamed, as we almost went off the road. *It felt like the Myth Mobile was about to roll over!* Then suddenly Uncle Hayden gained control, and pulled over to the side of the road.

"What in the heck was that?" Dad asked in shock,

shaking his head to wake up.

Uncle Hayden was really upset as he replied, “I don’t know what happened! It was as if something completely took over the RV. I just couldn’t control it!”

There was silence for a moment, then everyone unbuckled as we went outside to look around.

It felt creepy outside – it was completely dark, pitch black, except for the light coming from the inside of the Myth Mobile. You could actually hold your hand in front of your face and barely see it.

It was silent too. It gave me the shivers as I looked out at the never-ending nothingness. Even scarier was that there was not a car in sight, and as far as I could remember we hadn’t seen one in hours.

“I’ll get the flashlight!” Dad said.

“I’ll get mine too!” I exclaimed, following Dad back into the Myth Mobile.

Dad had an ultra-big, powerful flashlight that they used on the set for night tapings.

When he shined the light up and down the road there was nothing – just miles and miles of empty road.

“I’m scared,” Sissy whined.

“It’s alright dear,” Mom said, putting her arm around Sissy. “There is nothing to be afraid of.”

“Yes there is!” I said, as I put my face right up to Sissy’s. “Giant, man-eating aliens and extra-terrestrials that will suck the life right out of you!”

“Aaaaggghhh….!” Sissy cried, clutching my mother.

“Mick Morris!” Mom yelled. “You stop teasing her!”

“Alright, everyone back into the Myth Mobile,” Dad said. “Uncle Hayden and I are going to see if we can figure out what happened.”

I told Dad that I would stay outside and keep an eye on things. Sissy and Mom went inside. Dad and Uncle Hayden moved through the darkness toward the back of the Myth Mobile. I kept my flashlight focused on them until they rounded the corner and were out of sight.

I sat on the steps, hearing muffled sounds of Mom calming Sissy down inside the Myth Mobile. I could barely hear Dad and Uncle Hayden. Aside from that, there was a deadening stillness in the air as I stared out on the vast, black desert. I started to wonder about aliens – but it only lasted a few seconds until I heard a quiet squeaking sound.

I stood up and looked around, trying to see what it was and where it was coming from. It grew louder and faster, and sounded almost like something was spinning. It seemed like the sound was coming from the top of the Myth Mobile. I stood up, backed away, and shined my flashlight up to the top of the RV. Sure enough, there it was!

The satellite dish on the top of the Myth Mobile was spinning. Slowly at first, and then before I knew it, it was spinning like crazy! It had never done that before! In fact, it had never moved at all. *It wasn't supposed to move!*

"Dad! Dad!" I screamed with all my might as I ran toward the back of the bus. But no one was there! Dad and Uncle Hayden were gone! I was completely horrified!

Chapter Six

All of my fears had been realized! The next thing I knew, there was a blinding light shining right in my eyes! I couldn't see!

"Mick! Mick! What is going on?" Dad asked as he shined the flashlight on me.

"Oh my gosh! It's you, Dad! You are not going to believe this! Quick! Come with me!"

I pulled them around to the side of the RV. "Look! Up there!" I yelled, pointing to the top of the Myth Mobile.

Dad shined his flashlight up, then asked, "What? What's wrong?"

There it was; the satellite dish, sitting there, perfectly still.

"What am I supposed to be looking for?" Dad questioned.

"The satellite dish was spinning, it was moving like crazy!" I said.

"What?" Dad asked again.

"It must've just been shadows, and how could you see anything with your flashlight out?"

I started to tell him what happened – how the minute I shined my flashlight on the satellite dish the light bulb popped like a kernel of popcorn, but he was already walking back towards Uncle Hayden.

"Found the problem!" Uncle Hayden yelled.

I followed dad to the back of the Myth Mobile.

"Looks like we hit a patch of sand on the road. It must've made us lunge," Uncle Hayden said.

Sure enough, sand was covering the road.

"Well that explains that," Dad answered. "The wind must've blown sand over the road. Let's get moving! I saw on the map that there's a rest stop about 45 minutes from here. We can stop there for the night and get a couple hours of sleep, then get an early start. We'll be on the set by 4:00 a.m."

It sounds early – but 4:00 a.m. was our call time, so that shooting could start promptly at 7:00. "Shooting" is another word for filming.

We climbed back into the Myth Mobile, but I felt that weird feeling that something just wasn't quite right. I knew that I saw the satellite dish spinning. I saw it with my own two eyes! It was spinning like a top. What I also knew was that it felt like an unearthly force.

The one thing that Dad and Uncle Hayden failed to realize was that there was *no wind!* The desert air was dead still.

How could sand have blown over the road? If it had been there before we hit it, Uncle Hayden would have seen it!

It was all starting again, just like on past myth-solving trips. I could feel it. I was the only one who could.

Mom and Sissy had already fallen back to sleep. I really don't know how anyone could sleep with Sissy snoring. It was so loud, and she had this weird stuttering snore. It sounded like a pig that was hungry. She was making disgusting sounds, "Hhhuuggah...Hhhugggahh…" How annoying! And it was keeping me awake!

The Myth Mobile glided down the road and pulled into the rest stop. My bunk bed was next to the window. As I peered out the curtain, I could see a little bit, because the clouds had parted to make way for the moonlight, lighting up the barren desert.

It wasn't much different from where we had just been, and had that same weird feeling. It was completely empty – not a car in sight – just a couple of outhouses looming in the shadows. I knew this was one myth I was going to have to solve.

Suddenly I was startled, and could've sworn that I saw something zoom by the window. But I was tired. Maybe it was just my imagination playing tricks on me, or maybe it was a desert owl, or even a vulture looking for its next meal. *Or maybe a UFO looking for lost alien life? Worse yet, could it be an alien looking for human life?* As I closed my eyes and drifted off to sleep, I knew that my worst fears would soon be realized.

Chapter Seven

I woke up, startled once again by a shiny silver object floating past the window. I knew this time I wasn't just seeing things! This was it! I was going to be abducted by aliens!

I jumped up and almost fell out of the bunk bed, only to realize that it was a microphone boom being carried by the window!

"Whew!" I said, catching my breath and peering out the window. I saw that we were already on the set. The crew was there, scurrying around setting up for the filming. I must've slept right through the rest of the drive!

Then I heard a weird noise coming from the back of the RV. I looked around and realized that it was only Sissy still snoring like a little piglet.

I climbed out of bed and began to load my backpack. I wasn't going to be without my gear on this myth-solving adventure!

"Good Morning Mr. Spy man," Sissy said.

Oh no! I had awoken the serpent! I continued packing, acting like I didn't hear her, hoping that if I ignored her she would fall back to sleep.

"Going out alien hunting?" she snorted.

I decided that she was definitely more like a pig than a serpent, but she sounded like a pig when she slept – a ser-pig, that's what she was.

"Alien got your tongue?" she asked.

Ser-pig just wouldn't let up.

"Sissy, aliens are not something to joke about," I snapped. "And if you would have read the book I gave you, you would know that there is a definite possibility that we are not the only creatures in this universe!"

"Speak for yourself! I am not a *creature!* And you are going to have to prove it to me! So you just wait for me while I get ready, because I am going with you on your Man from Mars mission!" she said, laughing, then strutted into the bathroom and slammed the door.

That was it! I was outta there! In all the confusion last night, I had fallen asleep with my clothes on, so they would have to do today. I grabbed my gear as fast as I could and ran out of the Myth Mobile.

The minute I got outside the temperature changed a million degrees. It was so hot out you could fry an egg on the sand! But even though New Mexico was super hot, it was beautiful. The desert landscape was dotted with craggy rock formations, mountains, and cactuses, with a sprinkling of bright yellow, pink, and red cactus flowers. The sky was the bluest I had ever seen, with huge soft, fluffy, white clouds. Besides the beauty, there was something more to it – a mysterious feeling about this place that just couldn't be described.

I jumped, startled from my thoughts, when our boom operator Dennis tapped me on the back.

"Easy there, Mickers!" Dennis said. "How's it goin?"

Dennis Hinkleson was a really cool guy with wild-looking short red hair that stood on end. He loved to talk about myths for hours and hours, debating mysterious things and happenings. He was big and burly, and super strong. He had to be, since he was in charge of all the microphones and recording equipment. Dennis was so good at it that someone nicknamed him "Boom." Sometimes he would have to hold the mikes on large stands over the set for a really long time to get the tricky camera angles.

"Hey, Dennis!" I said. "Pretty cool place!"

"With some wild history here, my boy! So don't you be wandering off too far from this set," Dennis said with a wink. "We'll talk more about it later, fella!" And he was off to set up.

I never knew when to take Dennis too seriously – but what I did know was that he believed in legends and myths.

The rest of the crew was busy setting up. We were finally at the famous location known for its UFO sightings, where the actual flying saucer supposedly crashed in the 1940s.

While giant lights were being put into place on the set, Mom and Dad were finishing in makeup. Shooting always started promptly at 7:00 a.m., and it was already 7:30 – something was wrong!

That's when I overheard the assistant director say it was impossible that all of the batteries had been drained. He was arguing with the gaffer –the chief electrician – telling him that he had personally seen to it that they were charged last night. Little did they know their technical problems were just beginning!

But those problems would be tiny, compared to what I was on my way to face!

Chapter Eight

"Good morning, my handsome son!" Mom said as she planted a kiss right on top my head. I hated being kissed in public, but I just went along with it because I didn't want to hurt her feelings when she forgot.

"Hey Mom! Is Nathan here?" I asked hurriedly. Nathan Juarez was our director's son. He was 11, and even though Nathan was a year older than me, we were the exact same height.

Nathan was skinny and had pitch-black hair and freckles. He said the freckles were from his mom, who was Irish, and his black hair was from his dad, who was Spanish. Nathan lived with his dad in California, since his parents were divorced. His mom was a writer and his dad was a big time director, and they still were good friends. Nathan said they did that for his sake.

His dad had directed some pretty famous movies, but Nathan had no interest in Hollywood. He wanted to be something totally different, like a scientist.

He was a pretty cool kid and could figure out a lot of scientific things that I couldn't, and he spoke both English and Spanish. Nathan went to a private school full of rich kids, and loved traveling with his dad to the Myth Solver sets on school break. We were best friends, even though we didn't live in the same city. Nathan was more serious, but I could make him laugh a lot. We had a ton of stuff in common, so our parents let us email each other twice a week, and sometimes call long-distance.

We had been on a couple of missions together before and saw things that no one in the world would have ever believed. On our last myth-solving mission, Nathan and I were lucky to have made it out alive!

"I'm going off exploring, Mom," I said. I knew that I only had minutes to get out of there before Sissy caught up with me.

"What about Sissy?" Mom asked.

There it was. I knew they were all going to want me to hang around with her, but she would just be a pain, and would definitely slow things down.

"Not without me, you're not!" said a familiar voice. Nathan walked up and with his usual careful manner and said, "Let's go solve this myth!"

"You're on!" I said, as I turned and high-fived Nathan. We had emailed each other about our plan for this myth-solving mission, but Nathan wasn't sure that he would be able to make it this trip. I was thrilled to see him!

"Bye, Mom!" I said, flinging my backpack over my shoulder, and running with Nathan while we waved back at our parents.

Just then Nathan's dad, Miquel Juarez – walked up to Mom with a script. Whew! The director saved us!

Mom waved and yelled, "Don't you wander too far away, I need to be able to see you!"

"And don't forget to keep those walkie-talkies on and check in!" Mr. Juarez yelled.

We were already off and running and didn't hear Nathan's dad telling my parents about all the technical troubles that they had been having. So we didn't know that we were already headed for trouble.

The further we ran, the more dangerous it became. As we rounded the craggy, sharp, grey rocks just behind the first hill, I could have never, not in a million years, predicted the weirdest, strangest thing that would happen next.

Chapter Nine

"Look!" Nathan said, pointing to the top of a rock formation.

From where we were standing, it looked like there was a small person way up on the very top of the jagged rocks, about 500 feet away.

"I think it's a girl!" Nathan said.

Suddenly things became very weird. It was really hard to see, but it did look like a girl. In fact, by the size of it, it looked like – it looked like it could be *Sissy!*

"How totally strange," I said squinting in the bright sun. "I think that's my cousin that came with us! That's Sissy!"

"Well, what's so weird about that?" Nathan asked.

"What's weird is that she was in the Myth Mobile when we left!" I answered.

"OK, that is mucho-weird! But it must be her, who else would be out here?" Nathan asked, as he began to shout, "Sissssseeey!"

That instant the figure stopped frozen in its tracks, then slowly turned in a jerking motion to look at us. Then before we knew it, it turned around and began running again.

But not towards us – it was running away from us!

"What the heck? What is she doing?" I asked frantically. "We'd better catch up to her and whatever silly game she is playing."

It was getting hotter as the midday sun began beating down on us. The faster we ran up the rocks, the hotter it got. Sweat was running down our faces and we were slowing down. The next thing I knew, there was no sign of Sissy, but we kept climbing up the steep, sharp rocks.

"Whoa! Look at this," I yelled, reaching the top and looking down. "It's a giant crater!"

Nathan scrambled up to join me. We were both trying to catch our breath.

"Wow! I've never seen anything like it," Nathan panted.

By then I was busy guzzling water. I handed the bottle to Nathan and he chugged it down. We were so taken by the sight of this enormous hole in the ground we almost forgot why we had been running up the hill – until I looked down to my left and saw the tiny figure again, running right into the middle of the crater.

"Sissy! Sissy!" I shouted, as loud as I possibly could. "We've got to catch her! My mother will be furious if she gets lost!" But before I could finish getting the words out of my mouth I saw the most terrifying sight I had ever seen in my life!

Chapter Ten

There was a huge, white blinding flash of light, and then it was as if the ground just opened up. But what happened next was something that I will never forget! *The crater swallowed Sissy right up! In a split second she was gone, missing – disappearing into the dust and tumbleweed that swilled madly in the huge, deep circle!*

"Oh no! Sisssssey!" I screamed. Even though I wasn't crazy about her she was still my cousin, and I sure didn't want anything bad to happen to her.

"What?" I heard, in Sissy's voice.

Oh no! She was talking to us from underground! *What was happening?*

"I said, *what*?" her voice came again!

Nathan and I looked at each other, then slowly turned around to find Sissy standing right behind us! We both jumped a mile!

"And please give me some of that water," snapped Sissy, " I am so thirsty from running after you guys! Have you two lost it, or what?"

She grabbed the water bottle from Nathan's hand.

"You kept shouting my name while running away from me!" Sissy hissed.

I felt all of the blood rush from my face as I tried to get my thoughts together. Nathan just stared at her, pointed toward the crater, and stuttered, "Weren't you just over there?"

"Yeah, right!" laughed Sissy. "What, is the desert sun getting to you two already? I bet you've been hallucinating lakes and stuff too!"

"Nathan's not joking Sissy! We thought we were chasing you, and then you just disappeared into that crater!" I exclaimed, feeling a lump rise in my throat. Because if that wasn't Sissy, then who was it? Better yet, *what* was it?

"Well, I am clearly not in the crater!" Sissy barked at me, then totally changed her tone of voice as she turned to Nathan.

"Nice to meet you Nathan. I am Sissy, short for Cecelia Grace Areilia Kordell. The Aurelia name I added myself because I just think that… "

Sissy's voice trailed off and her expression changed as she stared at the ground near her feet. Her face froze with a look of pure fear and shock.

There it was! Right before our eyes! Evidence! Proof that we were not seeing a mirage caused by the desert heat! *There really had been a tiny being running away from us!* And here were teeny, tiny little odd-shaped footprints in the sand to prove it – footprints leading down the other side of the hill in the rock and sand, to the crater. Sissy looked back up at us, quiet and pale.

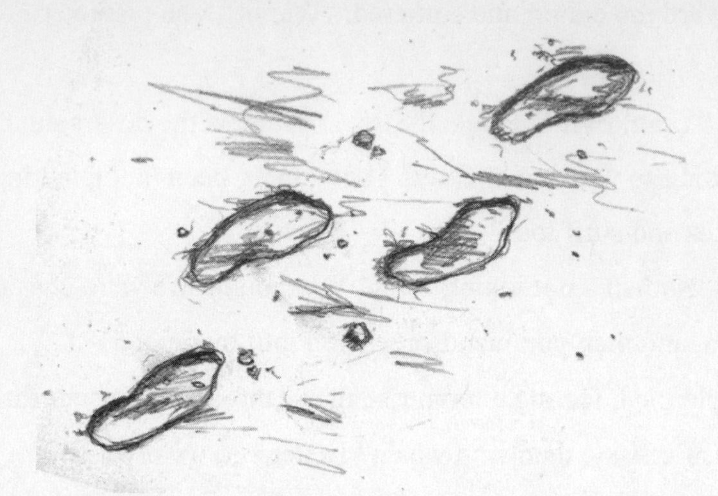

We all just looked at each other for a moment, then back at the footprints, until I said, “C’mon, you wanted to come along Sissy. If that was an alien we were chasing, then we are going to get to the bottom of this. This is one myth that is going to be solved!”

We started down the hill towards the crater, but we certainly couldn’t move as fast as whatever it was that we had been chasing. The rocks were sharp, and the sand sank away beneath our feet. The gravel made our descent unsteady, and there was prickly cactus everywhere. We had to be careful not to lose our footing as we inched our way down.

“Mick, come in Mick!” Mom’s voice startled me so much I lost my balance. Nathan saw me slipping, grabbed my arm and stopped me from falling down the steep ravine!

I regained my balance and struggled to reach for my walkie-talkie.

"Mo..mo…mom, hi! Over," I stuttered, trying to sound as casual as I could.

"Tell her what we saw! Tell her what we saw!" Sissy squealed in the background.

"Shhhhh! Be quiet!" I snapped.

"Mick, I am your mother, and I will not be quiet! You know better than to talk to me like that!" Mom hollered through the walkie-talkie. "And why exactly do you want me to be quiet anyway? Over."

I glared at Sissy with a look that said,

"*If you open your mouth you'll be in more trouble than you know,*" while I gently replied, "Oh, Mom, I didn't mean you…uh…we found…uh, a little creature, yeah a creature, and we didn't want Sissy to scare it out of its nest. Over."

"What kind of creature? In a nest?" Mom asked. "Mick, you be careful. No playing with desert snakes or lizards or any other creatures, do you hear me? Over."

"Oh…OK I won't! Over," I replied.

"Good, and keep that walkie-talkie on. Touch base every hour, and please be sure to keep an eye on Sissy. Over." Mom answered.

"Will do. Over," I said, trying to sound as totally normal as possible. *But what was about to happen to us was anything but normal –in fact, what was going to happen was completely paranormal.*

Chapter Eleven

The walkie-talkie must've shot a signal into the air, because the minute I clicked it off we heard this weird humming sound, coming from the crater. Without any warning at all, bright blue neon beams of light began shooting towards the crafter from the sky! As they glowed they began to form a triangle, and giant gusts of wind and dust blew everywhere.

"Get down!" I screamed. We scampered to hide behind the bigger rocks. Nathan was close enough that I could scoot next to him, but Sissy was still a few feet behind us.

"What's going on?" Sissy blurted out at the top of her lungs, trying to see what was happening.

"I don't know," I said. "Just get down!"

It was too late. Swirls of dust and tumbleweed were flying everywhere. The sky grew dark, and a huge, black triangular ship emerged. It was like it just came right out of the earth. Or so I thought – I couldn't really tell where it was coming from because of all of the dust and wind.

I didn't know if it was coming from the sky, where the blue beams streamed from endlessly, or from inside the ground, where the sand and dust swirled like a tornado. It didn't really matter though, because what we were seeing was absolutely unbelievable! It was a gigantic, threatening, black triangular ship hovering just above the massive crater.

Then in a blink – in a sleek, effortless move – it zoomed right towards us.

"Oh my gosh! What is that thing?" Sissy screamed as she stood up.

"Get down!" I said in a fierce whisper, trying to make my way over to her. But the rocks gave way beneath my feet and the mysterious, black ship was almost right above us.

"It's coming our way!" Sissy screamed.

"Sissy! Please, please get down!" I pleaded. My heart was pounding in my chest.

She stood there for a moment with her mouth open, just staring up at the ship. When she finally decided to slowly kneel down, *it was too late!* The ship was right over her. When I tried to move toward her, Nathan pulled me back and covered my mouth.

The next thing we knew the neon blue light beams wrapped around Sissy's wrists and yanked her up in the air, then stopped. For a few seconds she was just hanging there, suspended in mid-air! The next thing we knew, she was being pulled toward the ship!

A huge black panel slid open on the bottom of the evil looking spacecraft. Inside, there were green shadows lining an angular space – and it was swallowing Sissy! In a split-second she disappeared into the scary, dark ship, and the panel quickly folded shut. *Within seconds the ship vanished at warp speed into the sky.*

Chapter Twelve

Nathan and I sat there stunned, unable to speak. We couldn't believe what just happened! Sissy was gone! Pulled right into some mysterious ship! What was I going to do? And it was true! It was all true! Unless the United States Military was flying some sort of supersonic ships and picking up small girls in the desert for no apparent reason, the story of Roswell and Area 51 was real! I sat there in complete shock until I felt a tug at my arm.

"Now what, Mick?" Nathan asked timidly.

"Well, we have to get Sissy back! That's all there is to it!" I whispered.

"But how?" Nathan asked.

"That's a good question, and I don't exactly know. But I suppose we can stop whispering," I said out loud. "And not by just sitting here."

"Oh, c'mon Mick…you're not saying…." Nathan said, his eyes widening.

"Yeah, I'm afraid I am. I don't think we really have a choice," I replied.

Nathan swallowed and nodded. We slowly got up from behind the rocks, picked up our gear, and looked around. Once again, we began to carefully navigate our way down toward the mysterious crater.

When we got to the bottom of the canyon we tried to move as quietly and carefully as we could, slowly inching our way closer and closer. We were hiding behind any rock or piece of tumbleweed that we could find, even though the tumbleweed didn't prove to be a very good hiding place since you could see right through it.

I pulled my compact metal detector out of my backpack, unfolded it and turned it on. Within seconds it was going off at rapid speed.

"What do you think?" I asked Nathan.

Nathan picked up a handful of soil and rocks, eyed them very closely, and shook his head.

"No, not enough mineral here," he replied.

We slowly moved closer to the crater. The closer we got, the more the metal detector clicked and buzzed. At the perimeter, the metal detector went crazy, with the red needle on the meter flipping back and forth wildly.

"But there's nothing here!" Nathan said, confused, looking carefully at the sand.

I was just about to agree with him when there was a ripple in the air – like a wave – and the entire atmosphere seemed to be opening up. It was like a giant can opener was prying open a piece of the air!

But that was impossible!

How could the air have a second layer? *But it did.* I was so terrified, I was trembling. We slowly began to back up, but it was too late. It was as if a huge door began to open in the middle of nothing – and right in front of us! This huge, shiny silver, metal square door with the word STAL-ITE on it! Right before our eyes!

I felt Nathan shaking beside me as we crouched behind tumbleweed and watched the mysterious door slide open. Then an enormous ramp lowered to the ground – a ramp that led into an unending blackness and blinking lights. We were so terrified we couldn't move! We had just seen my cousin zapped up. Now what was in store for us?

There were aliens running down the ramp! They were coming right for us! Before we knew it they had formed a circle around us and just stared! We backed together in the middle of their circle, and all I could think was *this is it! This is the end of the line for us. We're going to be attacked by aliens!*

Chapter Thirteen

It felt like we were on another planet – a planet filled with aliens. Short aliens, only about three feet high with a grayish-green skin, enormous heads, and giant, slanted black bug eyes. They wore one-piece jumpsuits in shiny metallic gold and silver that looked like they were made of liquid when they moved. There was some sort of emblem on their chest and another one on their left leg.

I felt Nathan shaking beside me as he said, “I think that

I have to go to the bathroom."

And even though I was scared out of my mind, I didn't want to scare him even more, so I replied, "Well, you could ask them use their restroom."

"Mick!" Nathan snapped. "This is absolutely no time to be funny! Now what do you propose we do?"

But it was too late! The minute we started talking one of the aliens walked briskly toward us, carrying a black box that he had aimed straight for my face. We began to cover our faces and shrink to the ground, terrified, but the little alien held the box up to his tiny round mouth and made some warbling sounds into it. What came out of it was:

"Do not be afraid, People of the Earth! We mean you no harm. I am a Nougou, and I am the negotiator for my people."

"OK, whew, we aren't dead yet! How's that for news, Nathan? They are willing to negotiate! OK, we got some communication going here now! Whew!" I was so relieved that I couldn't help babbling for a moment.

"Not clear, not understanding 'Whew!' What is 'Whew' talkative Earth person? If Earth people would…" he began, then stopped when the emblem on his leg lit up.

He turned to face another alien who waved at him in a weird manner, as if he was running for a beauty contest. The alien that waved had a tall silver collar with glowing orange trim that stood up around his neck. It was something that none of the other aliens had.

All the aliens shifted their feet for a moment, doing the exact same waving move, then returned to their standing positions.

Again the negotiator spoke into the box: "Please excuse my informality. Cram Earthlings 200 years."

We stared at him questioningly.

"Cram Earthlings 200 years. Please respond now," he said again.

"I…I…I…we…we…Um…well….err…" I was desperately trying to speak.

Then Nathan elbowed me, "You see, we…"

"S…S…S…Sissy!" Nathan stuttered at me.

That reminder was all I needed. One alien or 200, I had to find my cousin and save her!

"Where is my cousin?" I demanded. "I want her back and I want her now!"

"Your cousin is not with our kind," replied the negotiator.

"What do you mean? I saw you beam her up like it was nothing, and zoom off," I said.

"Negatory," he replied.

"Then who did? No! Don't even tell me there is another kind of alien here! Don't even begin to tell me that!" I cried.

"Alright," the negotiator replied calmly.

"Alright what?" I demanded.

"You don't want me to tell you, so I won't," he responded.

"That was a figure of speech," I said.

"I do not understand speech with shapes," he answered.

"Mick! Plain and simple English – that's what we need here if we are going to get them to understand us," Nathan snapped.

"OK, look – my cousin, a relative, was taken away by a big black ship," I said.

"Yes, I know," the negotiator replied.

"Well, then can you tell us anything about that? Or can you help us get my cousin back?" I asked.

"Anything about them," he replied.

I was getting really frustrated so I said, "OK, I get it! I have to be very clear with what I say here!"

"I have never seen Earthlings become clear," he replied and continued, "Please let me explain. Our worst enemy – the Lizenbog – took your Earth kind. I will help you get your relation back, but in turn you must help us."

"Anything at all!" I yelled. I was confused, and relieved at the same time. But what I didn't realize was just how dangerous and life threatening "anything at all" was going to be!

Chapter Fourteen

As he explained, we began to understand what was happening. The Lizenbog were their arch-enemy. The Lizenbog hated the Nougous and wanted to take over the Nougous planet. They would stop at nothing to do so.

The Nougous were a peaceful, highly advanced alien life form. They lived 60 light years away and could travel that time in hours with their warp speed capability and ultimate knowledge of coordinates. They could also cloak their ship in a shield of invisibility, which explained why we couldn't see them when the metal detector was going crazy. It was the same reason the door opened up in mid-air. The outside of the ship had been invisible!

The Nougous had come to Earth when they received a signal from the ship that had crashed to Earth back in 1947! It was all beginning to make sense now – well, almost.

The Nougous told us the evil Lizenbog were rogues and thieves, traveling from planet to planet seeking out food, water and energy sources. When they completely wiped out all the resources of a planet, they would move on to the next planet.

When the Nougous received the signal from Earth, the Lizenbog were hovering in the galaxy just above the Nougous planet – just like they always did while trying to get into the Nougous planet.

The Lizenbog couldn't break into the Nougous planet because the Nougous had advanced technology. The Lizenbog picked up on the signal being sent from Earth, and waited in the outer limits, listening with their reptile-like sensors. When the Nougous spaceship took off, they attached themselves to the ship with their leaching capability and rode silently to Earth on the back of the Nougougian ship. They would never have been able to get to Earth without the Nougous warp speed capability.

So now they were here, and they had taken Sissy as a hostage!

"We can't waste any more time! I've got to save my cousin!" I exclaimed.

"Fine, then follow me!" the negotiator replied, as he did a weird hand motion. Then every alien slapped the emblems on their chest, and in that instant, the entire Nougougian spaceship was visible!

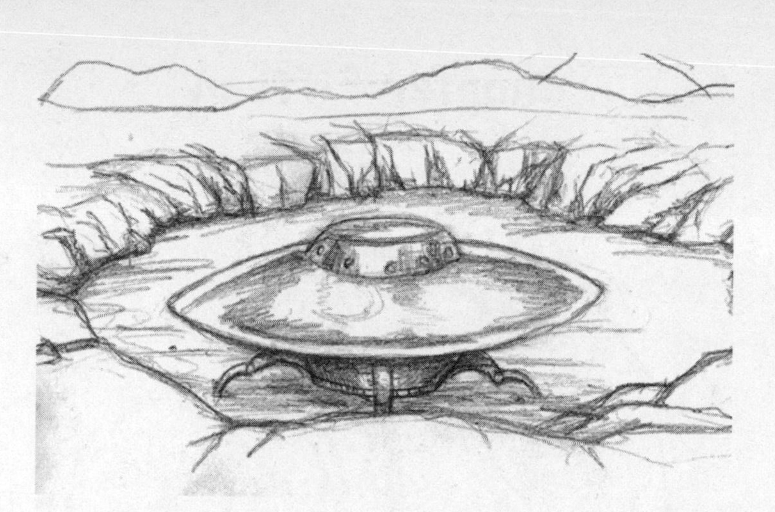

It was a huge, round, shiny silver craft, so large that it filled the entire crater. It was also very thin, with wild curves circling the outside. Strangely, the metal looked exactly like the shiny metal that I had seen in UFO books about Roswell!

"We are receiving a message," said the negotiator as he spoke into the little black box. Then he slapped the emblem on his chest again, in a weird code.

All of a sudden a huge screen appeared from out of nowhere, right in front of us! It was almost like we were at the movies, but outside in the desert! But, if we were at the movies, this was one horror show I didn't want to see. On the screen was the most horrible, bizarre looking creature I had ever seen in my life!

Chapter Fifteen

It was a Lizenbog! It looked like a giant green lizard that was half-human, half-alien! It had a human-shaped body with slimy scales covering it and a long, thick tail. Down the middle of its back was a line of giant orange, knife-sharp, pointed spikes. It had claw-like hands with three fingers and long black nails that looked like a raptor claws. The feet were the same. Its head was oblong with piercing, angular orange eyes, a long thin mouth, and just two small black holes for a nose.

Nathan and I were scared stiff when it began to speak.

"Nougoooouuuu! You will give us your power *now!* If you do not agree, we will sacrifice the Earth girl!" shrieked the Lizenbog, while orange drool poured out of its mouth.

My stomach turned. The voice sent shivers up and down my spine! It sounded like it had sandpaper in its throat.

"Give me back my cousin!" I screamed at the top of my lungs.

"Ahhh, as feisty as your female species, I see! But your female is not so talkative now, is she?" replied the Lizenbog.

Suddenly Sissy was onscreen. Aside from the frightening green alien, it was the most terrible site that I had ever seen in my life! Sissy was trapped in a huge glob of lime green goo-that looked just like slime. She was covered from head to toe, and there was only a small round opening around her face. They had placed a thick piece of tape over her mouth so that she couldn't scream or talk. The goo was totally gross, as it dripped and churned around her. She was unable to move – it was almost as if the goo was alive, and keeping her prisoner. The look in her eyes was one of sheer horror.

"Oh no!" said Nathan. "What now Mick?"

"I don't know, but we better think fast!" I whispered.

"The Nougou said that they would help us, so we better talk to them, without letting these lizards hear."

"Yessss, what are you going to do, Meeek?" screetched the Lizenbog leader. He was standing right next to Sissy.

"Nothing," I replied, as coolly and calmly as I could.

"Nothhhiiing?" the Lizenbog squealed back, in a pitch so high it hurt our ears. "Then we will keep your Earth human and dissect her for our human studies!"

"Fine," I said, as Sissy's eyes widened with fear. I knew that there had to be some way to let her know to hang on, that we would save her, but without the Lizenbog knowing. I had it!

Sissy had a habit of chewing gum, stretching it out of her mouth, and then putting it back and chewing again. I thought it was the most disgusting thing I had ever seen in my life, and she knew it.

"Nathan, do you have any gum?" I whispered hurriedly.

"Gum? *Gum?* At a time like this you feel like chewing some gum?" he asked.

"Yeah! Give me some gum!" I said, clenching my teeth as I talked.

Nathan quickly dug in his pocket and found a ratty old piece of gum covered with lint and fuzz. He tried to get the lint off it as he handed it to me. I shoved it in my mouth and chewed it as fast as I could, while stalling the Lizenbog.

"So – just how fast does that piece of tin travel?" I asked the Lizenbog.

"I do not understand you, Earthling! You are more self-centered than I thought! You have one more chance to regain your family relation back safely," the Lizenbog snapped.

Perfect. I had stalled long enough. The gum, as gross as it was, was now stretchable.

"No thanks," I said as I pulled it out of my mouth and put it back in.

Sissy had caught on. She knew that my playing with chewing gum was a message to her. I could tell by her face she was relieved, but she also knew that she couldn't let on.

"Then you have chosen her fate!" yelled the Lizenbog leader.

In a split second the huge movie screen was gone. It had simply vanished, and Sissy with it. I had a sick feeling in my stomach and I knew that it wasn't from the gross gum! I knew that we had a very, very short time to save Sissy.

Chapter Sixteen

The Nougou were all staring at the sky. Nathan and I looked up to see what they were staring at – and there it was. The scary black triangular ship was visible now, and hovering straight above us. It was watching, waiting, and threatening.

The negotiator approached me and did what I assumed to be some kind of wave for us to be silent and to follow them. Nathan looked frightened, but he knew as well as I did if we didn't go along with them we would never see Sissy again.

We followed the small gray-green Nougous toward the same area where the ramp they had marched down had been.

We were now completely surrounded. Then, instantly, the huge ramp opened up again – right out of thin air.

The Nougous walked up the ramp and into their ship, and we followed silently. I was so frightened that my throat was completely dry, and I swear they could hear my heart beating. Nathan was scared too. His face was pale, but he looked straight ahead, completely amazed at the alien technology. This was the type of thing that he had dreamed of building one day.

The ship was filled with hundreds of tiny Nougou aliens. We could feel their stares and knew that they were talking about us. We followed the long, curving corridor into the main chamber of the ship.

We were guided to massive metal screen chairs with high backs. When we sat down, seat belts automatically criss-crossed over us, and the ship immediately began to lift off the ground. Lights and sirens sounded. The leader of the Nougous sat right next to us with the negotiator on the other side. The negotiator translated what the leader said, and I couldn't believe what I was hearing!

We were now in a completely, invisible ship! They had the power to cloak themselves in shields of invisibility at any time. Before I knew it, the spacecraft dipped and we were at warp speed. It seemed that the ship almost turned sideways at times, and in a split-second it felt as if we were suspended in space. They did this to throw off the Lizenbog.

Suddenly it looked as if the floor of the ship was giving way! Huge metal panels shaped like flower petals rapidly folded over each other, revealing a glass floor just below our feet. We had zoomed and turned, and now we were floating just above the Lizenbog ship!

"This is so cool!" Nathan exclaimed. "Can you even believe it?"

"Not yet I can't," I replied, fearful for our lives, yet thrilled that we actually knew that aliens were no myth!

Just then, a blinking light flashed three times, and a binging sound went off. Aliens around us began to unbuckle and move from their seats. The only belts that didn't unbuckle were Nathan's, and mine.

Now I was scared. Had we been captured too? Was all of this just a trick to kidnap us? We tugged and pulled at our belts while the small aliens watched us with their big, angular black eyes! I was more frightened than ever!

Chapter Seventeen

I felt like I couldn't breathe. Nathan was pulling at his belt too. Then he suddenly stopped. He went pale, stared straight ahead, and mumbled, "Mmmick, mira!"

"Nathan! English, please," I whispered.

"Mira! I mean look!" said Nathan.

I turned to look. A huge creature – looking like it was half gorilla and half frog – was heading straight for us. It was enormous – twice the size of an average man, and snorting. It had an angry look on its face. It made me sad for a moment, because the snorting reminded me of Sissy's snoring.

This weird looking creature was dressed like a Viking, all in old brown leather with lots of metal buckles and bands with pointy spikes. It was carrying a large toolbox in one hand, and what appeared to be a giant laser gun in the other.

I squirmed in my seat as the negotiator motioned him towards us. The beastly looking thing then grunted some weird sounds at the negotiator.

Nathan and I looked at each other, fearful for our lives. Then the negotiator quickly picked up the black box and spoke into it.

"Do not fear, Earthlings! We must unlock those belts with a locking gun."

The creature was now at our sides, snorting. He held the gun over our heads and pushed it into a bolt in the middle of the two chairs. Our seatbelts immediately released.

"Oh yeah, OK, a locking gun. I should have known," I said, rolling my eyes at Nathan.

"Yeah, makes sense to me! And exactly why did we need to be locked in to begin with?" asked Nathan. "And just out of curiosity, why aren't those seats automated?"

"They were the only seats on the bridge available at warp speed for a larger species such as yourself," replied the negotiator. "Remember how important it is to buckle-up. We never planned on having visitors in our most technologically advanced ship, The Stal-ite."

The negotiator warbled some sounds at the mammoth gorilla-frog Viking-thing, who picked up its tools, looked us over, shook its head and grunted away.

As we stood up the seats immediately pulled back behind us, folded up, flipped over into a completely flat surface and reshaped themselves into a table. From overhead a large tube lowered to just above the table, then what looked like a blueprint out of some strange material, shot out of it, landed on the table and unrolled itself.

"Ok, now that's what I'm talking about!" Nathan said joyfully.

It was a blueprint, but it wasn't on paper, and it wasn't in English. It looked like hieroglyphics.

"Hieroglyphics!" I shouted to Nathan.

"Yeah? Maybe…" Nathan answered.

"Don't 'cha get it?" I shouted, as I pulled my backpack off and began digging for my book about Roswell. I found it, and quickly flipped to the page where I had read about how the metal that had crashed on the rancher's land had mysterious markings that looked like hieroglyphics.

The minute I opened the page to show Nathan, the negotiator grabbed the book out of my hands. He started screaming in some weird alien language and showing it to the leader of the Nougous.

The leader began to sway from side to side, making the same weird alien chant. Then they all swayed from side to side. It was as if we were at a concert of aliens. They were chanting at the top of their lungs, "Charrra, Charrra, Charrra!"

It was clear that they were extremely happy. The negotiator approached me with the book and yelled into the box, "Nougougian! Nougougian!"

The book was now proof to them that the signal they had been receiving really was from their ship!

It was in that exact moment that I decided to forget about being afraid and trust the Nougous, no matter how frightening it became. And it was just about to get a zillion times more frightening!

Chapter Eighteen

We almost lost our balance as the Nougou ship took a sharp, angular turn. Looking down at the huge black triangle of the Lizenbog ship, I saw that we were only a few feet above it. If it moved suddenly, the Stal-ite did the same.

We could see the glow of the neon blue beams as they quickly bounced across the desert from the Lizenbog ship. They were combing the desert for the missing Nougougian craft.

The negotiator and the leader began to point to the blueprint, as the negotiator spoke for his leader once again: "Now that we are certain that the lost ship is ours, it is of great importance that we get to whatever was left of it."

"I don't really know how to say this, but you must know that there is no existing life on that ship. It's been almost 60 years," Nathan said as quietly and gently as he could.

"We do realize this," said the negotiator.

"Then what is the importance of your mission? Isn't it more important that we save Sissy first, before they hurt her?" I questioned.

"You must know that if the Lizenbog get access to that signal, they could find the secret cylinder that is sending it. That cylinder contains all of our most highly advanced secret knowledge and super-sonic energy plans," said the negotiator. "The cylinder is sending us the message from the lost ship. It has the commands to our invisibility shields, as well as our technology to travel at warp speed by light years. If the Lizenbog get to it before us, they will gain access to our planet, and Earth as well. Life as we all know it will be over!"

"May I ask why you would put all of that technology on a cylinder and a ship to Earth?" Nathan questioned.

"We thought that Earth was a peaceful planet and that we would trade our technology for your health discoveries. We cannot survive as long as Earthlings. But we were careless in our thoughts and research of humans. We failed to realize that humans couldn't get along with each other, let alone communicate with alien life forms."

I saw sadness come over the negotiator, but then he quickly snapped out of it. It seemed that the Nougous all felt the same thing at the same time – if one was sad, they all were.

"But why do you need us?" I asked.

"The Lizenbog are searching the area with their blue laser beams. The beams are broken by contact. We are small beings, and do not have the body strength to break the beams. That is where you can help us in the recovery of the cylinder, and in turn we will save your relation. "

Somehow it all made sense, and in that instant I knew that I would have to take the greatest risk of my life. The only way I could save Sissy was to rescue the cylinder and save the Nougous – and Earth as well.

So, we began our life-threatening mission.

Chapter Nineteen

We were strapped into super-sonic, jet-propelled backpacks, then positioned against a clear door that looked down into a large slide –just like the big curving slides they have at water parks. Huge silver hooks with long metal wires hooked into the ship on a metal runner held us in place. The door to the slide slowly opened; we remained connected to the ship.

The Nougougian leader was speaking rapidly while the negotiator translated, telling us that we would be released the second the Lizenbog beams lock onto the signal from the cylinder.

The jetpacks would then self-propel, while the Nougous did the steering and controlling from the ship. They would guide us to the ground of the desert as the signal cylinder was located and pulled up to the Lizenbog ship. It would be our job to grab the cylinder by snapping the blue Lizenbog beams. The Nougous would then propel us back up to the ship. Timing was everything! *If we didn't grab the cylinder quick enough the Lizenbogs would get it, and the world as we know it would be over!* And I would never see Sissy again!

We were lucky that the Lizenbogs had no idea we were there. Thank goodness for shields of invisibility! With the advanced Nougougian x-ray technology, we were able to see right inside the Lizenbog ship. We were keeping an eye on Sissy, just to make sure that they weren't hurting her before we could save her.

I had to admit that I had been wrong about Sissy. I thought that she was just a silly, timid girl. But she was tougher than I knew, she wasn't just a girlie-girl like I had thought. And we were going to save her.

This was a myth-solving mission in which our every move had to be perfect. Timing was of the utmost importance, because while we saved the cylinder and distracted the Lizenbogs, the Nougous would use their one last ultra-powered laser shot to beam Sissy up through the Lizenbog escape hatch.

"This is it!" Nathan said. "You cool?"

"Cool as a cucumber," I replied. "Ready?"

"Ready as if my name were Freddy!" Nathan answered.

We both knew that we were as scared as we could be, but being courageous for each other and for our mission to save the Nougous – and our own planet.

We continued watching the desert floor as the blue beams swept across the ground. Suddenly one beam stopped and locked onto a spot. Then another beam zoomed in and locked on the same spot, and then another. This was it! Our jetpacks immediately ignited!

Chapter Twenty

At first it was a loud rumble. Then the jetpacks went almost silent as we slid down the curving slide. When we were nearly to the end of the slide the belts released and the hooks gave way. We were propelled into the air!

Whooo Hooo! My stomach did flips! I held on tightly to the handles on either side of the armrests that supported me. Nathan was right by my side, and we were both staring straight ahead at our target. We were flying towards the ground so fast! It felt like a hundred miles an hour.

I couldn't think about anything except getting my hands on that cylinder. *But what if we missed our target? What if the Lizenbog caught us?* I tried to put those negative thoughts out of my head as I glanced towards Nathan. We were wearing shiny silver helmets shaped like the head of the Parasaurolophus dinosaur, and could talk to the Nougous and each other through them. We looked like alien spacemen ourselves! Nathan was totally focused on the ground as we zoomed towards it.

We could see that there was a rumbling – then the dirt began to erupt! Something was ready to explode out of the ground! We were almost there, swooping towards whatever was being slowly unearthed.

Suddenly, it was beginning to show! I was just feet away from being able to grab it. There it was, popping out of the ground, the smooth, round, silver cylinder. It was bigger than I expected, and the top of it glistened in the hot desert sun. I was closing in on it as it began to move faster and easier out of the ground. I was just five feet away, and Nathan was right beside me! We were both leaning forward, ready to grab it, now that it was almost completely out of the ground. Steady, steady – Oh no! I was coming in too fast, and Nathan was turned at a weird angle! We only had this one chance – this was it!

We were now in the scope of the Lizenbog. They could see us, and if we missed, it would be over. The Lizenbog would rule every planet in the universe. Life as we know it would be over. Two feet away! No! We were gonna miss it! *The Nougous were bringing us in too fast*. I didn't know what to do. If only my arms were a few inches longer. Nathan and I weren't going to connect. This was it! I knew what I had to do. I quickly let go of a handle and unbuckled the first buckle of my jetpack. Nathan glared at me, fiercely shaking his head and screaming, "Nooooo! Noooo!"

I couldn't look at him. I leaned in. We were just seconds away from impact. The silver cylinder was almost completely out of the ground. I was just inches away from Nathan as I was rounding the cylinder, and I was still going to be too far off. I could hear the Nougougians in my headset, and they sounded upset.

Then Nathan started screaming, "What are you doing man? Stop it! You are going to get yourself killed!"

"It's me or Earth, buddy! I gotta take this chance – get closer to me," I screamed. "I need your help, pal! This is our only chance!"

I unbuckled the second strap. This time the harness jerked. That was it! I lurched forward, with only one strap holding me into the jetpack. I could feel the jetpack slowly sliding off. It was so powerful, and now it was unbalanced and shaking violently. I grabbed Nathan, who held onto me with one hand while trying to steady himself with the other. My jetpack was so loose I had no choice. *I had to let it go! It was my only chance of getting close enough to the cylinder!*

I undid the last buckle, and the jetpack went soaring away. It took off with such force that it threw me violently to the ground! I landed right on top of the cylinder – at the exact moment it was pulled out of the ground by the Lizenbog beams! The cylinder was heading right for the ugly black ship – but with me on it!

Chapter Twenty-One

Nathan began screaming at the top of his lungs, "I'm coming for you! Hang on Mick! I'm coming for you!"

There was nothing I could do but to hold onto the cylinder for dear life, while being slowly pulled toward the Lizenbog ship!

I could hear the hum of Nathan's jetpack right behind me. In my headset I heard him say, "Hang on Mick! Don't give up! I'm coming to get you! Get ready to let go of that thing!"

"What?" I screamed. "I'm not letting go of anything!"

"Si! I mean –Yes, you have too!" bellowed Nathan. "I'm right behind you! Without the force of your jetpack, we won't be able to break the Lizenbog beam."

"I'm not giving up!" I yelled back. "I will not let go!" I was terrified, but I knew that there was no turning back now.

"You always were as stubborn as a bull!" said a girl's voice –a familiar girl's voice!

It was Sissy!

"I'm catching up to you Nathan – hang on Mick! The

girl has joined the party! I've had about enough alien goo to last me a lifetime!" Sissy yelled happily.

Within seconds Sissy was right next to Nathan, and together they started gaining speed.

"Right on!" Nathan yelled.

But it seemed that the faster they went, the faster the beam pulled the cylinder towards the Lizenbog ship. The scary black triangle was getting closer and closer, and the huge panel door was sliding open.

If the Lizenbog got their gruesome claws on the cylinder it would be over. It would be the end of the world!

Out of the corner of my eye, I could see Sissy and Nathan getting closer – they were just a few feet away from me.

"Hold your hand out!" Nathan hollered at the top of his lungs.

"We're almost there, Mick!" Sissy yelled. "Get ready to jump over to us!"

"I can't give up!" I screamed over the roar of their jetpack engines. "Just try to get over me – together we can break the strength of the blue beams!"

I could see Sissy and Nathan lock arms, giving the jetpacks more force. Within seconds they were zooming right over my head. We were about fifty feet from the black ship, and I could see the Lizenbogs climbing into small pod ships!

Sissy and Nathan were hovering above me in the blue beams, which were losing their strength, and starting to break up.

One was gone! Then two! They needed to get in the way of the third beam, but every time they tried, one of the other beams would re-engage. It was a constant shifting. Then suddenly they formed a circle over my head, and all at once the blue beams disengaged! Nathan and Sissy had managed to break them apart! But the moment they did, the cylinder and I were like puppets whose strings had just been cut! We were plummeting to Earth! *We were going to crash from thousands of feet in the air!*

Chapter Twenty-Two

This was it! I was going to die trying to save the planet! I was tumbling and turning, over and over, but held onto the cylinder with all my might! As I fell, I could hear Sissy and Nathan's screams, and the roar of the jetpacks as they tried to make their way towards me.

Suddenly, there was a jolt, as if something had grabbed me. Then, another jolt, and another! I was flipped upright and once again hooked by the blue beams.

"Oh no!" I screamed. Once again, the beams had locked on and I was being pulled toward the Lizenbog ship. But this time I was closer to the ground. Sissy and Nathan were rocketing down towards me.

"Here we go again!" Nathan yelled. "Yipppeee Kaaayy Yeh!"

This was a great time to become a cowboy, I thought to myself. Nathan was waving something wildly over his head. His belt! He had taken off his belt!

“Lock arms again!” Sissy screamed. “We’re taking this puppy home!”

It looked like we were going to crash! As the beams pulled me up, Sissy and Nathan were zooming straight down for me! But that wasn’t all! The Lizenbog pod ships were descending from the mothership! Nathan and Sissy were just feet away from me now.

“Mick! Can you free up one hand to catch this when I throw it to you?” Nathan asked.

“Yeah!” I yelled back to him.

“Ready, Sissy?” Nathan yelled. “On the count of three!”

“Ready!” Sissy hollered.

This was it – this would be our last chance! The Lizenbog pod ships were heading right for us. I was a goner if this didn’t work.

“One –two –three!’ Nathan and Sissy yelled together, and Nathan flung the end of the leather belt my way.

“Got it!” I yelled as I caught the buckle, which I hooked onto one of the myth-solver spring hooks on my backpack.

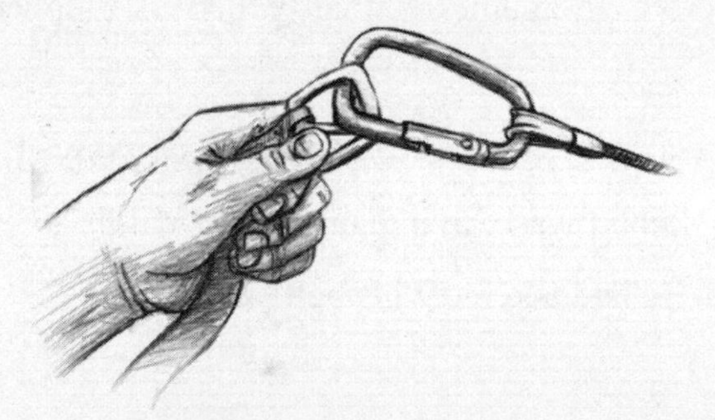

At the same time, Nathan and Sissy held onto the other end and formed a circle over me.

One blue beam! Two blue beams! Three! As they broke the last blue beam, I felt myself lunge once again, but this time I was suspended in mid-air by the belt. They were pulling me up at the same time they were zooming towards me. Before I knew it, we were all in a circle, heading down – thirty feet, twenty feet, ten, five – and then we crashed to the ground!

Chapter Twenty-Three

We hit the ground with such impact we were sent rolling into a gorge. I could feel cactus cutting at my clothes. Dust and sand was flying everywhere. I was trying to stop rolling and I knew that Sissy and Nathan were too.

Finally the hill leveled out and we slowed down. Then the weirdest thing happened! We all just came to a sudden stop – like we had hit an invisible force field.

But it didn't matter how or why, because there was no time to waste – the Lizenbog were not far behind!

"Nathan! Sissy!" I screamed. They were a few feet away from me and had managed to stop rolling down the steep hill. "Over there!" I pointed towards a very small, round, dark hole. It looked like an opening in the side of hill. It had to be a cave!

I held the cylinder tightly with my left arm, and scooted towards them with my right. One wrong move and I would be rolling down the steep hill again.

Sissy and Nathan were struggling to remove the harnesses of their jetpacks, which had shattered when we hit the ground.

"Nathan! Sissy! You guys alright?" I asked.

"Yeah! How 'bout you?" Nathan replied.

"Fine, thanks!" I said.

"Yeah, me too," Sissy said. "But we don't have time to talk! I just have to tell you that when the Nougous rescued me, they used their last source of power. Until we get that cylinder back to them, they do not have the energy to beat the Lizenbogs. They have nothing left except for the invisible shield, and they're depending on us to save them and the planet!"

I could hear the Lizenbog approaching on the other side of the hill.

"Well then we are on our own. Wrap an arm around the cylinder and hold on tight. We've only got seconds to get to that cave before the Lizenbog get to us!" I said.

We scooted as fast as we could towards the small, dark opening in the side of the ravine, trying to work together so we wouldn't lose our balance and fall hundreds of feet down.

"Ouch!" Sissy screamed.

"What is it?" I asked.

"Cactus in my….in my…oh, never mind!" Sissy said. "It's nothing compared to alien pod goo all over me!"

As we moved closer to the cave we could hear the frightening hum of the pods just over the other side of the gorge.

"Oh no!" said Nathan. "They'll see where we left the jetpacks!"

"We can't worry about that now," I said.

We were just a few feet away from the cave entrance, and had reached an area where could stand up. We jumped quickly to our feet – still hanging onto the cylinder – and ducked into the small, black, round entrance of the cave.

It was dark, damp and scary, but it was amazing too. It was this huge circular looking tunnel made completely out of rock. There were stalactites everywhere.

"This cave must've been here for thousands of years," I exclaimed.

"Wow, it's incredible!" Nathan said.

"Pretty creepy, if you ask me!" Sissy added.

As we looked around the massive cave, I fished the flashlight out of my backpack. Luckily I had changed the bulb, and it all made sense to me now – why the light bulb had popped, why the satellite dish had spun around madly – it was all from the energy sources of the alien ships.

I wondered for a minute how things were going back on the film set, then shined the flashlight deeper into the cave.

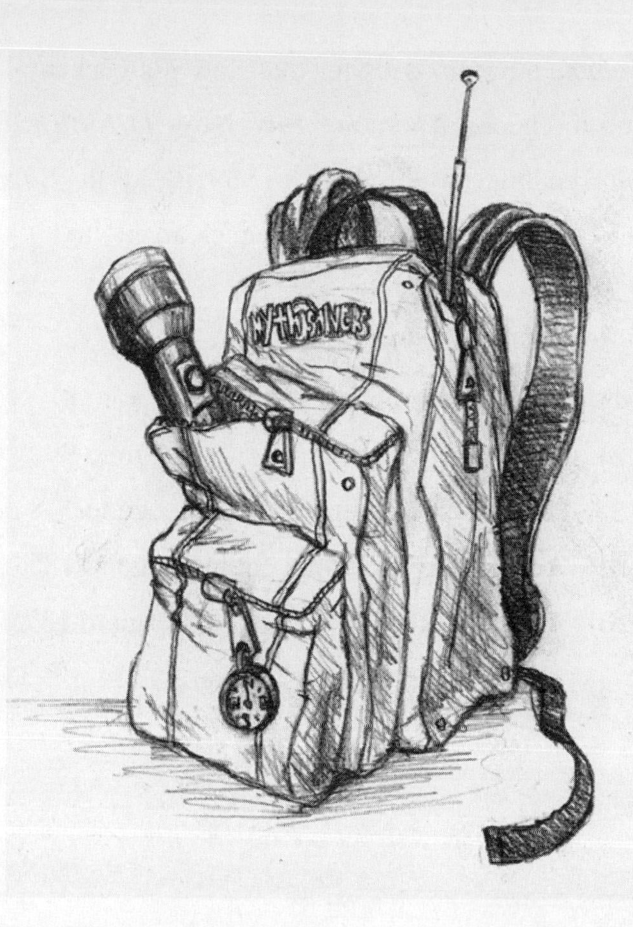

The Lizenbog pod engines were growing louder – they were getting closer!

"C'mon! We've got to hide!" I whispered. We ran further in to the cave and ducked down behind some tall crystal stalagmites. There was nowhere else to run, and nowhere to go! We were trapped, and the Lizenbog were just a few feet away!

This is where the story ends for me. Now it's your turn! It is up to you to choose. There are ***Five Ways to Finish*** this story. Each ending to this Mick Morris Myth Solver Adventure is different. It's up to you to pick an ending:

1) A normal ending……………… go to 81
2) A super silly ending……………go to 99
3) A very scary ending……………go to 118
4) An exciting superhero ending.....go to 185
5) A very short ending…………....go to 187

Chapter One - Normal

We scrambled to hide behind a giant rock as I looked up at the cave formations. The number of stalactites – looking like enormous, dripping rocks hanging from the ceiling – was amazing. I couldn't help but stare at them.

"Mick, now what?" Sissy asked. "And what are you looking at?"

"Hold on a sec!" I replied, still staring up at the stalactites.

"Mick, c'mon man, we gotta figure out a plan!" said Nathan.

I looked down at the cylinder at that exact moment, and couldn't believe my eyes!

"I think I just did!" I exclaimed. "Look at this! The name of the Nougous ship was the Stal-ite, right?"

"Yeah." Nathan replied, while Sissy nodded.

"And if you look above, we are sitting under enormous stalactites!" I exclaimed.

"Mick, somehow I am just not in the mood for a geology lesson right now!" Sissy exclaimed. "And what are stalactites exactly anyway?

"Those huge hanging things up there that look like rock sculptures dripping from the ceiling – but listen up," I said. "Can you see what is etched into this cylinder? Look close! Here's an A, a C – and a T! *ACT!* Do you see it? It's the same name as the Nougous ship!

"So what was the name of the Nougous ship?" asked Sissy.

"The Stal-ite! Just like those!" I said as I pointed above my head. "S t a l a c t i t e – like *stal-ite!* Only missing the three middle letters: A-C-T! The three letters that are written on this cylinder! *This is it! This is our map outta here!* It all makes sense now. The Nougous were edging us over this way with the jetpacks! They were leading us to this cave! They must've got transmission before their ship crashed in this valley some 60 years ago! That ship didn't crash trying to land! It crashed after take-off!" I yelled.

"You could be onto something here," Nathan said as he looked over the cylinder. "You're right! Then that's what they were trying to tell us when they kept saying…"

"Cram Earthlings 200 years!" Nathan and I said at the same time.

"When *who* said *what*?" Sissy asked, wrinkling her eyebrows in complete confusion.

"The Nougous kept saying, 'Cram Earthlings 200 years,' and we didn't know what they were talking about!" Nathan replied.

"What they were trying to tell us was that they had been studying Earthlings for 200 years!" I said, finishing Nathan's sentence.

"That's awesome…I think," Sissy said. "But if we don't use that cylinder, and figure out a way to get out of here – we're gonna be history!"

"She's right," I said excitedly, knowing that this was just the breakthrough that we needed.

"OK, look at this!" Nathan said. He was examining the cylinder with a magnifying glass he had dug out of his backpack. "Here is the connection with the name of the ship, and it looks like hieroglyphics – but it's actually a map through the stalactites!"

"You're right!" Sissy said, as she pointed at the stalactites that were on both the cave ceiling and the cylinder.

"We're gonna follow this map to get out of here. Let's go!" I said.

Nathan and I put our backpacks on, but Sissy just stood there frozen, with a look of horror on her face. Then she screeched, "Are you crazy? You aren't actually thinking of going further into this cave are you?"

"We have to, Sissy!" I said, as Nathan and I studied the cylinder and stalactites.

"But…" before Sissy could finish her sentence, we heard the buzz of the Lizenbog pods approaching the opening of the cave. "OK then, lets get going!" Sissy screeched.

We ran into the blackness with only my flashlight to guide us.

Chapter Two - Normal

We were running at a pretty good pace, trying to avoid cavern pools that were a glowing, shiny green from artic algae, and stalagmites that grew up from the ground, instead of down. But even worse than that, every once in a while huge, ugly, black bats would take a dive at us, and we had to run through spider webs that were the size of doors.

It was like we were on a giant game board – and we were the pawns, trying to follow the rules of the game to get home.

Once we got further into the cave and away from the Lizenbog we stopped to catch our breath. According to the encoded map on the cylinder we still had further to go, but we had come to a fork in the cave. We had to choose which way to go – right or left. But the cylinder showed a dead end.

"The map ends here," I cried.

"I think it's to our left," Nathan said.

"I don't know," Sissy added. "It looks to me like the path curves the other way."

"All I know is that we have to choose the right way," I replied. "Look around, there has to be some other clue in this cave! There's something we're missing."

I shined the flashlight up and down, but there was nothing.

Suddenly Sissy grabbed onto my hand. Normally, I would say "ooouuuuu gross girl germs!" and shake her off –but she was different than I had thought, and now an important part of the team.

"Look, isn't that lime green sparkly rock pretty?" she asked, as she led me over to the rock and held my flashlight hand steady on it.

"You know, just when I think that you are really cool – you go completely squirrley-girley on me!" I said.

"Oh stop your whining!" Sissy said huffily. "Look at the rock, will ya?"

"OK, the rock *is* unusual," I answered, feeling frustrated.

Then it hit me. "Wait a minute!" I said. "That rock doesn't belong in this cave!"

"Duh!" Sissy said.

The rock was completely different from anything else. There were no other rocks like it at all! It was just sitting on top of a large boulder like someone had put it there on purpose!

We walked over to it together, keeping the flashlight on it. When I tried to pick it up, it wouldn't budge.

Seconds after I touched it, there was a loud cracking sound, and an enormous boulder in the middle of the cave began to move!

There it was! It was the path that we had to follow! And there was light coming from behind it!

We ran toward the entrance to the path, hearing the Lizenbog right on our trail. They were right behind us!

Chapter Three - Normal

We ran towards the lighted opening as fast as we could, and were inside within seconds.

What we saw once we entered the passageway was startling! There was an enormous octagonal-shaped glass room, reaching thousands of feet up to the top of the cave! It was glowing from the inside and had clear panels all connected together at the sides. Inside, we could see a shiny, stainless steel floor and a huge computer lined with hundreds of buttons, knobs, controls, and switches.

"Amazing!" Nathan whispered.

"What is this place?" Sissy asked.

"Our ticket to saving the planet and ending this Myth Solver mission!" I replied hurriedly.

We slowly approached the huge glass room. Then I was shocked when I saw, in big bold letters on a mammoth circular steel button it read **A**lien **C**ave **T**akeoff –ACT! This was it! We were going to save Earth, the Nougous, the

Universe – and ourselves! I put my hand on the huge steel button and pressed it.

Nothing happened!

"Look!" Nathan yelled as he pointed to another button on a small silver panel at the bottom of the door. He pushed that button and a section of the door automatically lifted. Inside was what appeared to be the exact mold of the cylinder!

The next thing we knew there were strange orange lights bouncing off the glass, and a loud hissing sound. But before we could even turn around Sissy was screaming! The orange reflection had come from the evil Lizenbogs eyes as they slithered into the secret room! There were hundreds of the horrible lizard-like aliens, just staring at us!

As they hissed, they began to move from side to side, slowly approaching us! Their mouths opening and their black forked tongues flicked at us. They were lifting their grotesque, sharp black Lizenbog claws, getting ready to tear us apart!

"Quick! Put the cylinder in!" Nathan screamed.

Sissy began tugging on the door handle into the glass chamber while I scrambled to put the cylinder into the mold.

"It won't fit!" I screamed. The Lizenbog were heading straight for us.

"Turn it over!" Nathan shrieked. "Hurry, before we become lizard's lunch!"

"Hurry, Mick!" Sissy screamed.

Chapter Four - Normal

The cylinder slid in. There was a clicking sound, and when Sissy hit the huge button on the door it slid right open. We ran inside and the enormous glass door quickly closed behind us, just seconds before the Lizenbog got in.

The computer boards lit up, blinking like crazy, and a loud siren sounded – Whoop! Whoop! Whoop! The huge octagon-shaped room began to turn. Metal floor panels were moving in opposite directions. We were losing our balance! Suddenly, huge seats rose up from the floor.

"Grab a seat! We're taking off!" I screamed.

"Oh my gosh!" Sissy cried, as she and Nathan jumped into seats.

I freaked out when seat belts came out from the sides and automatically buckled us in, but anything was better than staying in the cave with the Lizenbog!

"Here we go!" Nathan screamed.

The room began to turn and lift off the ground, and the dark cave ceiling started to open. Bright sunlight blinded us.

The room was spinning faster and faster, like a carnival ride, as it lifted and spun quickly towards the bright blue sky.

"Look!" I yelled, pointing to the Lizenbog, who were angrier than I had seen them. Their orange eyes were shining an evil red. Some were climbing up the cavern walls to catch us! Others heaved boulders at the glass-like ship, but they just bounced off.

The ship was moving at hyper-speed as we reached the top of the cave. Suddenly a huge shadow fell over us – it was the Nougous ship! Within seconds the spinning glass octagon jarred up out of the cave and attached to the Nougou mothership with loud clicks and locking sounds. The two ships were connected and secured.

I looked back down as the cave roof closed. The entire cave exploded and crumbled, with all of the Lizenbog still inside!

"The Lizenbog are trapped!" I screamed.

"YEAH!" we all cheered.

Then Nathan pointed and screamed, "Look over there!"

Through the clear panels of the ship we saw a huge flash of light. The Lizenbog ship folded up into a single line, and then just *disappeared into thin air!*

We had done it! We had defeated the Lizenbog!

Chapter Five - Normal

Our seat belts released as a panel opened above us. We slowly stood up, as the Nougou leader and negotiator came toward us on a stairway that just appeared in front of them as they stepped down. Other Nougous in jetpacks circled around our glass ship, getting ready to release the silver cylinder from the compartment.

The excited Nougou leader held up his hands, wiggled his fingers, and began speaking to us in Nougougian.

Nathan, Sissy and I just looked at each other as the negotiator translated.

"We cannot thank you enough, Earthlings! You have risked your lives to rescue the cylinder, and in turn you have saved us all."

"Not a bad trade," I said happily.

"Not bad at all," Nathan said. Sissy nodded and smiled.

"For that, we will reward you with your own miniature energy capsule," the translator said, as he handed me a tiny replica of the cylinder.

"Awesome!" I said, as I took the miniature cylinder and carefully put it in my backpack. Then we all started to wiggle our fingers back at the Nougous. The three of us started to crack up!

Suddenly I heard my mother's voice over the walkie-talkie. "Mick! Mick? Where are you? Over," she said.

"Uh – excuse me just a minute please," I said, as I grabbed my backpack and found my walkie-talkie.

"Yeah Mom? Over." I answered.

"You've been gone all day, I was getting worried. We've just wrapped up," Mom replied.

"No need to worry – we're just out here saving the Universe! Over," I answered.

"Very funny Mick. C'mon back, its dinnertime. Over," Mom said.

"Be there in a few minutes! Over and out," I replied.

"OK, out," Mom said.

Within seconds we were gliding above the New Mexico desert, away from crushed cave filled with the hideous Lizenbog. What a myth-solving mission this had been! Now we knew the truth about whether alien life existed. As I looked out over the sagebrush-covered landscape, dotted with cactuses and craggy rock formations, valleys and ravines, it was hard to believe what had happened to us. The sky was an incredible swirling mixture of purple, blue, orange and pink. I could only stare up at it.

"Touchdown!" Nathan hollered, as the ACT ship slowly descended to the desert sand.

"Yippee!" Sissy yelled, as the large, clear door slid open. We grabbed our backpacks and were quickly out of the ship. Seconds later, the craft lifted completely into the Nougou mothership. We waved, and I wondered if they could even see us.

Then there was a flash of light, a streak across the sky – and at light-year speed, the Nougou were gone.

Chapter Six - Normal

We climbed to the top of the ravine, where we could see the ranch and the film set. As tired as we were, we ran toward it happily. Mom, Dad, Uncle Hayden and Nathan's dad all came to greet us.

"Wow, what have you guys been doing all day?" Mom asked.

"Looks like you might have been out Myth Solving!" Dad said.

"Uh…uh…no, not much…uh not really…" I said, as slyly as I could.

"Not much? Not really?" Sissy said intensely. Nathan and I both covered her mouth and pulled her away.

"We sure are hungry!" Nathan said loudly.

"Yeah, we're going right for the buffet!" I chirped in, heading towards the set and dragging Sissy with me.

Just as we turned our backs Dad said, "Now just wait one minute!"

We froze in our steps. They knew something was up! We were caught.

"I have news for you, Mick," Mom said.

Maybe they discovered aliens too, I thought to myself. I slowly turned around and said, "Oh, that's cool, what is it?"

"We aren't going home!" Mom replied.

"We're not?" I asked, trying to sound as casual as I could.

"Nope," said Nathan's dad. "There's really nothing here, and we've finished shooting under schedule, so we've been reassigned."

Nathan stepped closer and asked, "Reassigned? You didn't get a story here?"

"Same old news here," Dad answered. "The alien landing may or may not have been a hoax. It's hard to tell, lots of mixed facts and no real leads."

"Oh, I see! So then where are we off to now?" I questioned.

"Bluff Creek, Oregon," Mom said. "We're headed to the Pacific northwest."

"That's cool!" I replied.

"Sounds exciting to me!" Nathan said.

Sissy nodded and added "Uh, yeah – exciting."

As we all headed back to the set for dinner I knew that "the Northwest" could only mean one thing. This would be more than a Myth-Solving mission, this would be a dangerous trek! We were on our way to solve one of the biggest myths *ever*!

We were going on a search for Big Foot, which could only mean one thing…big trouble!

The End

Chapter One – Silly

We only had minutes to get away from the Lizenbogs as we looked inside the cave. It was painted neon purple, and we knew that purple wasn't their favorite color it would only make them madder.

"C'mon! This is way too disco! Follow me, and do just what I do!" I yelled.

We did a Conga line dance out of the neon cave. I laid down on the ground and started rolling down the steep ravine again. Sissy and Nathan did exactly what I did. As we gained speed, we sang a song until we suddenly hit something.

"Ouch!" Nathan laughed.

"What is *this?*" Sissy asked.

I was holding onto the silver cylinder for dear life, when I suddenly bounced into the same thing that Sissy and Nathan had hit.

We thought for sure that the Lizenbog had caught us, but when I looked up, I saw we had been stopped by an enormous volleyball net that was hundreds of feet long, but only about three feet high. I started to crawl over to Sissy and Nathan, but then I realized I could just stand up and bounce my way over. BOING! BOING! BOING! We all began bouncing sideways.

"This is better than cleaning my room!" Sissy yelled in a deep voice.

"I know!" I replied. "Gonzo!"

"Gonzo!" Nathan yelled. We were bouncing our way across the net.

"Look! I see another cave!" I said.

"Good! Let's go the other way!" Nathan hollered.

"I think we should keep rolling down the ravine," I said.

"I'm in!" Sissy screamed.

So we hopped over the net and started rolling down the steep hill again, getting sand and gravel in our hair and ripping our clothes on cactuses.

By the time we got to the bottom, the Lizenbog had spotted us and were after us again, so we stood up and waved at them.

Nathan gave them the peace sign and started to rap, "Yo, Yo, Yo Yo…"

Once we were sure that they saw us, we started to run away as fast as we could. Sissy was so slow that we took turns giving her piggy-back rides while she held on to the precious cylinder. We were exhausted by the time we finally got to one of the huge rock formations that looked like a giant school bus.

We ran around to the other side of it, hoping to find a door so that we could get in and drive away. But when we saw what we saw, even though we weren't quite sure what it was, we realized we would be safe. Now everything made nonsense.

There it was – a whole herd of black and white cows sitting in a circle in a clear spacecraft that was shaped like a teepee. The cows sat Indian-style on their cow butts, holding hands. It looked like they were meditating. *But they weren't! It was way worse than that! It was enough to make you cough up a hairball!*

Chapter Two – Silly

They were trying to force out farts!

Then one of the cows – the king cow – looked at us and said, “We thought you would never make it!”

I knew he was the king cow because he was wearing a crown.

“Hop on,” he said. “You know, like take a ride on our magic circle!”

Two of the cows scooted over to let us on, and we saw that they had been sitting on round, open holes. As they scooted over, we heard sounds like *pppffft... ppffft*. Sissy, Nathan, and I covered our noses as we walked to the middle of the circle and sat down.

"Hold on! It's going to be a bumpy ride!" said another cow, wearing a circle of flowers on her head. Every one of the cows had some kind of hat on.

The cows held hands. They scrunched up their faces, while mooing and farting!

They were the loudest, smelliest cow farts you could ever imagine! Every time one of the cows farted, the plastic circle teepee ship lifted a little further off the ground, and we would all bounce. Within seconds we were lifting up into the sky. *As the ship took off, the cows kept farting away!*

"Fart-off complete!" King Cow yelled. They all mooed at the top of their cow lungs.

"Moo," Nathan said as he looked at me.

"Moo, Moo!" I replied.

"I love Hawaiian clothes!" Sissy squeaked.

"You're onto something there," King Cow said.

The plastic teepee spaceship was swiftly moving up toward the top of one of the giant Hoo-Doo's and Hassa-Foo's. As we got closer to the top it looked like a golf course. Sure enough, that's where we were landing. Once we touched down and scored six points, every one of the cows grabbed clubs and ran to the carts for a round of golf.

We followed the carts outside, still not believing what had just happened, when the king cow came up to us and said, "How 'bout a few holes?"

"Uh, yeah…I guess so," I replied.

He handed me a box of small, round donuts and said, "I'll be right back!"

Sissy, Nathan and I just stared at the cows, that were now driving the golf carts in circles.

"Vee are going for a round of zee golf!" mooed a cow with a French beret.

Then they all started yelling and screaming in Spanish.

"Ole!" screamed a cow wearing a jester's hat.

"Arriba!" howled a cow wearing a top hat.

The cows all started driving toward a tree, to bat at a lizard-shaped piñata. The next thing we knew, they were all hitting it with their golf clubs. It broke apart in seconds, and tons of green grass started to pour out. The cows munched on it wildly. When the piñata was empty, one cow got up on another cows shoulders. Other cows passed him buckets of grass to pour through the broken piñata.

"I feel like some tropical punch," Sissy said.

"I'm hip to that," Nathan giggled.

"I like lima beans," I said, jumping up and down.

A big gust of wind came up, and we could see the huge, dark, triangular Lizenbog ship coming up over the rocks. I clutched the cylinder under my arm looser. With everything being so totally unrehearsed, we almost forgot about the dangerous Lizenbog.

But the ship looked different. It now had bright neon lights on it, flashing different sayings like “Far-out,” “Daddy-O” and “I picked my nose today.” They spotted us, *and were heading straight for us! We were finished, and had better come up with something slow!*

Chapter Three – Silly

"Tally-Ho!" the cow with the top hat yelled.

"Jump on!" squealed some other cows. So we rode the herd back to the teepee ship. Once inside, the cows began the fart-off again, while King Cow mooed out directions.

"Steer this ship!" King Cow said to me.

"But how?" I asked, "There's no steering wheel!"

"Oh," he replied.

He walked over to a big closet and opened the door. Tons of stuff fell on him: tennis rackets, dolls, clothes – the closet was just filled with junk. King Cow bent over and picked up a crumpled old New Year's Eve hat that looked like a crown, and handed it to Sissy.

"Here, this is for you!" he said.

"Why, thank you!" Sissy replied, putting the crown on her head.

King Cow walked back to the closet and continued digging. He was so deep into the junk that for a minute we couldn't see him. The next thing he came out with was an old record player – something that our parents used for music before there were CD's.

He started to play some Hawaiian music on it, while all of the cows swayed back and forth doing the hula. The ship started dipping from side to side, and it seemed to help the ship get off the ground faster.

"Nathan, young man, what was I looking for again?" King Cow asked.

"A steering wheel, I think," Nathan replied, as he looked at me and blew his nose.

"Ahhhhh yes! And here it is!" King Cow said as he shoved a steering wheel at me. "Now you drive, Mick Morris!"

Even though the steering wheel was just a small, fake, red plastic toy – the kind that has the little sound effect buttons on the side – when I turned it, the entire ship turned too!

"Whoa, little buddy!" King Cow said. "Do you have your drivers license?"

"No, not yet," I replied.

"Bessie! You're on deck!" he yelled, and a little cow came running over to me, pushing a desk with an old typewriter on it. She typed something on a little piece of paper super fast, and handed it to me.

"Please sign here," she said, handing me a pen and pointing to a line on the paper. "Now look here for your picture, and say 'cheese'! She held a camera right up to my nose and snapped a picture. For a second I couldn't see from the bright flash.

"There you go!" Bessie said, shoving the paper at me.

She turned to King Cow, saying, "Now he has his driver's license."

It was a good thing, because we were just about to crash!

Chapter Four – Silly

I pulled back hard on the steering wheel, and we just missed crashing into a monkey. The Lizenbog ship was hot on our trail mix! Maybe it was because Sissy had been throwing breadcrumbs out of one of the open cow-butt spaces.

I tried to keep the ship headed in a straight line, but the little red steering wheel was hard to control. The ship was zigging and zagging! Nathan and Sissy helped guide me by calling out square dancing directions.

"And around we go, let's doe-see-doe!" Sissy yelled.

"Pull by – right and left thru, now bow to your partner," Nathan laughed.

The entire cow crew took a bow. They must've really worked up some gas by bending over, because they all ran back to their circles and let out some wicked farts. The ship immediately began to gain speed. Sissy gave Nathan and I giant chip bag clips for our noses. We put them in our hair.

"King Cow! They are catching up to us! What should I do?" I yelled.

"I have an ultimate moo-plan! Head on down to our volleyball net!" King Cow replied.

"Circle left and pass thru! I love Square Dancing!" Nathan yelled.

A cow with a tall blue and silver wizard hat handed Sissy a tiny, tiny pair of binoculars. When she opened them up, they grew huge. Sissy tried to hold them up while looking for the volleyball net.

"There it is!" she screamed, pointing with a foam finger.

"Yeah, Sissy's right!" Nathan hollered.

I slowly turned the ship while holding loosely onto the wheel. I was going to have to be very crazy while I guided the ship over to one end of the net.

Suddenly the ship started to shake! It was hard to hold onto the steering wheel while still holding onto the cylinder.

"Nathan! Sissy!" I screamed. "Don't come and help me!"

"Oh please let us help you!" Sissy yelled.

"Oh, OK," I replied. Within seconds, Nathan and Sissy were helping me turn the wheel.

"Cows to the ladders! Cows to the ladders!" King Cow crowed.

"What's happening?" I asked.

"Cows must've ate some bad grass," said King Cow. "The ship can't handle it, looks like were gonna crash!"

Sissy, Nathan and I looked at each other as we held tightly to the steering wheel. We feared for our noogies.

Chapter Five – Silly

The cows dropped four rope ladders out the sides of the ship, and began doing water-skiing poses as they climbed down. It was an awesome show.

"OK! Let's land this tilt-a-whirl!" I said.

"Turn just a nose hair to your left," Sissy said.

Nathan and I held tightly to the steering wheel. We were now only inches from the net, and the Lizenbog ship was getting closer and closer. The cows on the ladder suspended themselves – upside down while holding onto each other by ankles and tails – as they grabbed for the end of the net. *The Lizenbog ship was almost next to us.*

"I'll need fart gas in full take-off mode at the count of four!" mooed King Cow. "Mick Morris and Nathan Juarez, steer as bad as you can! Sissy, direct us to the flat breads!"

We all nodded, smiled and shook hands. I couldn't see how the plan might just not work! As the Lizenbog ship got closer, the King Cow counted.

"One! Two! Three! Four! What's the ship we're fartin'for?" he mooed.

The cows grabbed the net as the Lizenbog ship hit it. Nathan and I turned the ship with all our might and the ladder cows held tightly. The plan went successfully and Sissy guided us to a nutty landing.

Once we had safely landed, King Cow grabbed his record player and started yelling "Chihuahua! Chihuahua!"

Some of the cows ran to a trunk and started pulling out instruments. There were accordions, xylophones, trumpets and clarinets. King Cow yelled, "Let's MOOO!" and all the cows headed for the exit door and slid out of the ship on sleds.

"Once they're set up, we'll follow," King Cow explained. "We have to be very careful, or this could be the beginning!"

Sissy was so scared she started to moonwalk, and Nathan began to snort. I whistled for a second and then had to stop because my head was filled with cartoon bubbles.

Chapter Six – Silly

"The Lizenbog will itch through that net when they come out of their ship!" King Cow said.

"Correct!" said a cow in a motorcycle helmet.

"But they'll steal the cylinder and destroy the Nougous planet and Earth!" I howled like a coyote.

"Incorrect!" said a chef-hatted cow, as he banged barbeque utensils over his head. "Just watch!"

King Cow was peering through the giant binoculars. "It's time, they are all in place," he said, nodding to us.

I balanced the cylinder on my head, jumped on a sled, and slid out of the ship while hiding behind the cows. The door to the Lizenbog ship opened. It was a wonderful site to see the horrible Lizenbog slithering out. Sissy began to shake, because we could see the Lizenbog leader – the one who had been onscreen with Sissy when she was covered in gooey, green, gross, gopher guts.

He stared straight at us and hissed, "Give me that cylinder! There's no time like the present! I see London, I see France!"

"The present is passed, just like gas! And-a one, and-a two!" King Cow sang.

Polka music filled the air as the cows began playing their instruments. They were jammin'! Suddenly one of the Lizenbogs completely exploded! Bright pink goo flew everywhere – and then another one exploded. And then another! *Lizenbogs were popping into pink neon goo everywhere we turned!* The more they popped, the louder the cows played. More and more Lizenbog poured out of their ship and popped pink!

When the last Lizenbog slowly crept out of the ship, the last accordion note sounded, "POP!"

"It's over!" Sissy screamed.

"They're all gone!" Nathan yelled. "And my socks smell!"

I turned to King Cow who was pointing at the splattered pink Lizenbog goo. Other cows followed behind him, scooping the goo into wheelbarrows. The goo had hardened into what looked like chicken.

"You helped us! You helped us save the universe!" I said.

"So, I did," King Cow replied, with a shy look on his face.

"I just have one question," I said.

"What's that?" he asked.

"What happened to the Nougous? Where are they?" I asked.

"That's two questions," he replied.

"Oh, OK," I said.

"Anyway, they are on vacation in Hawaii," he answered.

"Oh, I see," I responded.

Just then I turned to see that some of the cows were rolling out grills and starting to barbeque the Lizenbog chicken-looking goo.

"Stay for dinner?" the chef cow asked.

"Uh…" I looked at Nathan, who was violently shaking his head back and forth. Sissy was gagging.

"Maybe another time," I answered. "We really need to get back to the show."

"We understand," said King Cow. "And if you ever need any cow actors…"

"We know where to look!" I answered.

We gave bear hugs to the cows and thanked them for their spots. They promised to deliver the cylinder to the Nougous. We handed it over to them and began our long skip back to the set of The Myth Solver show.

When we got to the top of the hill we looked back.

"That's strange, that looks like some Nougous," Sissy said.

"It sure does! And it looks like they're holding cow costumes!" Nathan replied.

"Ahhh, you two are just being silly!" I laughed.

The End of the Tail

Chapter One – Scary

"Here, take these flashlights!" I said as I handed them to Sissy and Nathan. "Let's go!"

I knew we didn't want to move one inch further into the dark, smelly, spine-chilling cave, but we had no other choice.

We had to get as far away from the Lizenbog as possible. The further we ran, the heavier the cylinder became, so we would stop and take turns carrying it. It was getting colder and darker. We were running through mucky, algae–filled puddles and gigantic, thick spider webs. The smell was awful! There was weird brown goo dripping off the walls and ceiling. But even stranger than that, it felt like someone was watching us – some kind of an eerie presence.

"Mick, Nathan! Stop!" Sissy said as she collapsed against one of the enormous rocks and bent over to catch her breath. She had been lagging behind us.

"I don't know about this, Mick! This is getting really creepy! Besides, how are we ever going to find our way out of here? And the smell – it's so gross, it's making me sick!" she moaned.

Nathan and I stopped running. We were out of breath too. We slowly walked back to Sissy. I put the cylinder down and knelt on the ground next to her.

"Sissy, I know you're tired and scared. So are we, but we don't have a choice. It's either this or be caught by the terrible Lizenbog, and you know what that means," I said.

Sissy lifted her head to look at me, but as she did, something caught her eye and she just stared up behind me. She had the most frightened look on her face, like she had seen a ghost.

"It's not that bad Sissy, really. There has got to be another way out. We'll find it, c'mon, we'll slow down," Nathan said.

Sissy's face had grown pale with fear, and she continued staring behind us. She slowly lifted her finger and pointed up. Nathan and I turned our heads to see what was freaking her out.

"No way!" Nathan screamed, and we both jumped.

There were hundreds of yellow eyes just staring at us!

"Bats!" I exclaimed.

Ugly, brown, hairy winged creatures with glowing white fangs covered the walls!

"That's what that disgusting smell and brown goo everywhere is! Guano-bat poop!" Nathan yelled.

"Ooouuuuu!" Sissy cried.

"But they don't look like your average, everyday, eat-a-few-mosquitoes bats!" Nathan said.

"No they don't, do they?" I exclaimed. "Let's move away – very, very slowly."

"I can't move! I'm afraid!" Sissy cried.

"So are we, Sissy, but we have to get away from them!" I said.

I carefully bent down to pick up the cylinder, keeping my eyes on the gruesome bats. They were watching our every move, and it looked like they were ready to attack us!

"Sissy get between us – we need to stay close together," I whispered.

We moved slowly, hoping not to attract their attention any more than we already had. But the minute we moved, we heard an ear-deafening, fluttering noise. The bats were coming right straight at us! *The bats had begun to chase us!*

We ran as fast as we could. Sissy took off so fast that she was 10 feet in front of Nathan and me! It was hard to see because these dreadful flying creatures were everywhere! *There were thousands of them chasing us!* They were in our hair, on our clothes! Nipping and biting at us, flapping their ugly wings in our faces!

"Run! Run! Just keep running!" I screamed at the top of my lungs, while shooing bats away from my face. And then it happened. I heard Sissy scream at the top of her lungs. I tried to look up to see her – but she was gone! She had disappeared! *She had just vanished...and this time it was for real!*

Chapter Two - Scary

"Sissy!" I screamed while Nathan and I pushed bats out of our way. "Nathan, where's Sissy?"

"I don't know…I don't know where she went…" Nathan stammered, swatting at more bats.

We could barely see where we were going as the bats continued to chase and attack us! We got to the spot where Sissy had disappeared.

"AAAAgggggghhh!" I heard Nathan scream! One second later, I knew why!

"Oh no!" I shrieked, as I felt the sandy floor of the cave vanish from under my feet! The next thing I knew, I was falling into a huge dark hole! There was a loud swooshing sound, and a swirling wind – it felt like a tornado! I was being sucked into some weird vortex that had spun open! *I was sliding faster and faster into a long dark tunnel while sand and gravel was whoosing around me!*

"AAAHHHHOUUUU!" Sissy screamed. THUD!

Then there was silence – until I heard Nathan yell, "OOOOUUUUUCCH!" and I heard a FWOOP!

"Ouch!" Sissy cried.

"AAAHHHHHH!" I screamed, sliding out of the end of the dark, sandy tunnel.

BAM! I landed right on top of Sissy and Nathan. We were all groaning in pain while trying to move off one another.

"You guys ok?" I mumbled, rolling onto the sand.

"Yeah, I think so," Nathan answered.

"Sissy? Are you alright? Sissy?" I asked frantically.

I couldn't hear her and she wasn't moving.

Nathan and I – along with the cylinder – had landed right on top of Sissy, and wherever we were, it was pitch black and we couldn't see a thing. We had all dropped our flashlights in the long, dangerous fall down the black tunnel.

"Ohhhhh….ohhh…" Sissy groaned.

"Sissy! Sissy are you alright?" I asked, feeling along the ground to find her.

The next thing I knew I was holding onto a leg!

"Let go of my leg!" Sissy snapped.

"Sorry!" I said. "I was just trying to make sure you were alright."

"Ouch, now let go of me!" Nathan yelled. "Let go of the back of my pants!"

"I'm not touching you!" I exclaimed.

"Me neither…" Sissy replied.

I continued feeling around the ground for a flashlight, and suddenly found one. I was startled when Nathan screamed, "Mick let go! You're scratching me!"

"Nathan, I'm over here," I replied, fumbling to turn on the flashlight. Thankfully, it worked! I shined the light towards Sissy and Nathan. Sissy was kneeling near Nathan brushing sand and gravel off herself. Nathan was sitting half upright. I looked around for our other flashlight.

"There's my flashlight!" Sissy said. "And there's the other one, near your feet Nathan!" She picked hers up and turned it on – thank goodness, it worked too! We both crawled over to Nathan and shined our flashlights around.

"What is this place?" Sissy asked quietly.

"I have no idea," I answered. We sat there completely freaked out by what had just happened. Wherever we were, it was really creepy. There was an eerie graveyard feel to it. Giant cobwebs were everywhere, far bigger than the ones in the cave above us.

"Exactly how big of a spider do you have to be to make webs that big?" Sissy asked.

"Pretty big…I think." I replied. There were all kinds of things sticking up from the ground – I could swear they were bones. Then something shiny caught my eye. The cylinder! It was just a few feet away. I walked over and picked it up, and as I did, things cracked and snapped under my shoes.

"OK, I'm happy to see that we are examining our surroundings and gathering up our stuff, but I still can't get up!" Nathan snapped. "And if your not holding onto me, Sissy, and your not holding on to me, Mick – then exactly what is?"

"Let me see…" I said. I bent down to look, and jumped a mile! Nathan was stuck! *But what was holding onto him was one of the most hideous things that I had ever seen in my life!*

Chapter Three – Scary

"What? What is it Mick? What am I stuck on?" Nathan asked excitedly. He was scared and desperately trying to wiggle free.

"Uhhh…I think…I don't know…let me see…" I said, as I swallowed. "Uhh…Sissy could you take a look at this?" Sissy had scooted away.

"Oh, I don't think so," Sissy said boldly.

"Sissy, please!" My voice cracked. My throat had gone completely dry from the horrible site. "Nathan just sit still for a sec!"

"Oh, alright!" Sissy snapped. She came over with her flashlight and immediately blurted out, "Oh how gross! It looks like a skeleton claw!"

"A *what?"* screamed Nathan. "Help me!"

"OK, calm down! Sissy, just hold the flashlight steady," I said.

Sissy kept the light on Nathan's back while I tried to free him from the hideous skeletal claw. It had cut into his back and hooked onto his belt. It was really stuck and I struggled to get it loose. It was hard to break free because it was attached to whatever it was that was still buried!

"OK, hold on, it's almost loose," I said, thinking to myself how odd it was that this thing had such a grasp on Nathan and his belt. He must have fallen on it just the right way and it snapped shut.

"Done!" I said, as I had managed to break it off.

"Thanks Mick," Nathan said, standing up and rubbing his back. "But it still hurts…"

"Let me see!" Sissy said.

"No way! You're a girl!" Nathan snapped.

"Well, gee, Nathan – thanks for letting me on that secret!" Sissy said sarcastically.

"Here I'll look," I said, lifting Nathan's t-shirt.

"Oh yeah, you got a wicked little cut from that thing. Don't move."

I dug into my backpack and found a small squirt bottle of hand sanitizer – something my mom always makes me carry. "Here, this might sting a bit."

"AAAAGGGHHH! A bit! Mick, that just felt like you ripped my skin off!" Nathan cried. "What in the world was I stuck on?"

We knelt down to look at the massive claw sticking up from the ground.

"It looks like a Lizenbog claw," Nathan said.

“Yeah it does!” Sissy agreed, shining her flashlight around. “But I just want to know how…”

“Were in a graveyard!” I yelled, *“A Lizenbog graveyard!* The claw that Nathan fell on was still attached to a buried Lizenbog body! We better get out of here!”

Something grabbed at my shoe when I started to get up. I pointed my flashlight to the ground and was shocked to see the sand moving all around us!

“Sissy…Nathan…look!” I shrieked.

They pointed their flashlights to the ground – the sand was erupting! Enormous black claws – with decayed, brown Lizenbog skeleton hands and arms with leftover pieces of dried Lizenbog skin – started poking up from the ground! Pointed Lizenbog skeleton heads gritty with sand pouring through them, but with their razor-sharp teeth and claws still intact, were pushing up out of their graves! *Dead zombie Lizenbog were coming back to life, and now they were after us!*

Chapter Four - Scary

It was the most freaky, horrible thing I have ever seen in my life!

"Oh no!" Sissy screamed in horror, as a zombie Lizenbog grabbed her foot. She kicked it off with all her might, and backed up towards me.

"Follow me!" I screamed at the top of my lungs. I bent down to pick up the cylinder, but two Lizenbog skeleton limbs were wrapped around it, and a terrifying skull was rising from the sand!

"Help! Help me! It's got a hold of the cylinder!" I yelled, hitting the sharp, skeleton claws with my flashlight. Sissy came running over – we pulled and tugged at the cylinder.

"Nathan, help us!" I screamed, shining my flashlight toward him. It frightened me more than ever when I saw that Nathan was laying in the sand, *and hundreds of zombie Lizenbog were halfway out of their graves!*

"Sissy don't let go of the cylinder! I'll help Nathan!" I yelled, running over to him.

"Nathan, are you ok? Get up, we gotta get out of here!" I screamed, yanking him up.

"Oh yeah, ok…" Nathan replied in a daze. Something was different about him. His eyes were glazed over, and he was out of it. I helped him up and dragged him along. Sissy was now in a tug-of-war with the cylinder and the horrible half-buried zombie Lizenbog.

We all grabbed onto the cylinder while I yelled, "Pull! PULLL!!!"

The cylinder broke free and we went flying backwards into more zombies!

CRACK, SNAP, CRUNCH! The sound of their dead brittle bones cracking as we fell onto them was nauseating!

I pointed the flashlight around the room. It looked like there was no escape!

"I see something!" screamed Sissy. "Over there!"

We ran toward a wall in this nightmare of a place, trying to jump over zombies coming up out of the ground, and Lizenbog skeleton zombie hands grabbing at us. Some of them were standing up and heading our way – hissing!

"Sissy where are we going?" I yelled. "It feels like we are running in circles!"

"Look! I knew I saw something! A rope!" she hollered.

Sure enough, there was an old, beat up, partially frayed rope just dangling from a hole in the ceiling. Luckily we managed to get to it, since there was no other way out of this sinister hole.

"Sissy can you climb it?" I asked in a panic.

"Yeah, just hold the bottom until I get started!" Sissy replied. I grabbed the bottom of the rope as Sissy shimmied up. Next, it was Nathan's turn.

"Go ahead Nathan!" I said.

He just stood there, looking confused.

"No! MY BACK HURTS!" he turned and screamed in my face.

Nathan and I had never yelled at each other before. Even if we had our disagreements we always talked about it, we were never, ever mean to each other.

"I know, I promise we'll get that cut fixed the minute we get out of here! You gotta climb Nathan! It's our only way out! We've only got only seconds!" I exclaimed. *I could see the Zombies making their way straight for us!*

Nathan reluctantly began climbing the rope, but something was so different about him and it frightened me. I had never known him to be irritable, especially at a time like this. I knew his back was hurting him, but it only looked like a small cut.

I grabbed the rope getting ready to climb, and then knew that I was in a ton of trouble. The rope was starting to fray.

Even worse, I knew that I wouldn't be able climb the rope with the cylinder! I was trapped!

Chapter Five - Scary

"Mick C'mon!" Sissy screamed from the top of the small hole.

"The cylinder!" I yelled.

"Leave it!" she screamed back.

Leave it? *Leave it?* Was she kidding me? There was no way I could leave it! I had an idea! I pulled open the frayed ends of the rope and quickly tied the two ends around the cylinder. I then tied a tight scout knot and hooked one of my Mick Morris clips on my backpack onto the knot in the rope that I had attached to the cylinder.

I began climbing with the cylinder hooked onto my backpack, but it was heavier than I thought it would be. It almost felt like it was pulling me backwards.

Chills ran up and down my spine when I realized that it wasn't the cylinder at all, it was one of the zombie Lizenbog that had grabbed onto my backpack and was pulling me backwards!

"Help!" I yelled up to Sissy, just as Nathan crawled through the opening.

"Hang on, Mick!" Sissy screamed, while she and Nathan tried to pull me up. I held on as tightly as I could, kicking at the zombies. I was getting dizzy from twirling around like a puppet at the bottom of the rope.

As I came back around again, I used all of my might to kick at a horrible zombie. CRACK!

I hit his skull so hard it went sailing off his body, knocking over more zombies! More were just a few feet away – I used all of my strength to climb up the rope, and suddenly I was so glad I had paid attention in gym class!

"Pull! Pull!" Sissy screamed at Nathan. The rope was starting to fray at the top, and I just hoped that it would hold on until I crawled through the hole. I kept focused as I grasped the rope and pulled myself up. I was inches from the opening now! *I had made it!*

I could see Sissy and Nathan through the opening. Nathan seemed even more irritated as he continued pulling me up.

"Now whatever you do, don't let go!" I laughed out of sheer nervousness.

I took one more look into the cave below and was shocked to see that the zombie Lizenbog didn't need any rope to get up to the ceiling of the cave! Hundreds of these horrendous bare-bone, lizard-like aliens were climbing up the sides of the walls! It was like a sight out of a horror film! They were snarling and hissing as they got closer and closer to me! The shock of it caused me to loose my footing! *Oh no! Just as I began to fall off the side of the wall, I felt another tug!* Not again!

Chapter Six - Scary

I was so relieved that the tug wasn't from another zombie grabbing onto me, but from Sissy and Nathan holding tightly onto the rope and pulling me up! I scrambled to grab on as I reached for them. Sissy and Nathan pulled me through the small opening, and I couldn't help but notice that Nathan's hands felt like sandpaper. He must have torn them up on the rope.

"Thanks!" I said. I quickly untied the knot and unclipped the cylinder from my backpack. "Now lets get this back to the Noguous!" I cried.

"But how? Which way do we go?" Sissy asked.

There were three paths to follow, and one of those would lead us right back to the Lizenbog outside of the cave. But now there were two types of Lizenbog that we had to deal with!

"We are just going to have to wing it!" I answered. "What do you think, Nathan?"

He lifted his head and just stared at me, then pointed to a path.

"OK, so there you have it, we'll go that way," I exclaimed. This time we ran so fast that our feet barely touched the ground. We knew that if we didn't move as quickly as possible, it wouldn't be long before the zombies would catch up to us.

That was an understatement – I could already hear the hissing getting closer. They were crawling out of their hole of a grave and were after us, and the cylinder!

"Hurry!" I yelled. "We're going to have to find somewhere to hide!"

As we turned another dark pass in the cave, we found a hidden crack next to a boulder.

"What about in there?" asked Sissy, stopping to point at the opening.

"We don't really have a choice, do we? Let's just hope there aren't any more zombie burial grounds!" I whispered. "They make bats seem friendly!"

We twisted and turned to fit through the small crack in the wall, which led into a tunnel. It was almost like a mini-hideout and we sat perfectly quiet, waiting for the zombies to go by. That was easy for Nathan, since he was no longer speaking to us.

"We should be safe here until they pass," I whispered.

We were scared to death as we heard slow, dragging footsteps and hissing sounds going right by the wall dividing them and us. Then there were some odd scratching and sniffing sounds. We sat huddled together in fear, waiting until they had gone by.

"I guess were safe now," I finally whispered.

"Whew…that was creepy," Sissy answered.

But not half as creepy as the next moment, when Sissy screamed at the top of her lungs. A skeleton Lizenbog claw broke right through the wall of the tunnel we were in!

It was trying to grab us! I leaned over and pounded on it with my flashlight. But instantly another zombie hand broke through, and another and another! One after another, more and more of these hideous skeletal zombie lizard claws were breaking through the wall. Horrible, vicious bones grabbing at us, completely cracking through the sand and rock!

We were fighting them off, hitting them with our flashlights, whacking them, as their bones would snap and crumble to the ground.

I was closest to the crack that we had managed to fit through and one of the zombies was trying to squeeze it's boney self through while I kicked at it with all my might!

"Get down!" I screamed, and just as I did, another claw broke through and pinned Sissy's neck against the wall! She was trying to pull the ghastly claw off, and gasping for air! I tried to reach up and help her, but just as I did, another one grabbed me by the foot and was started to pull me out!

"Nathan! Help Sissy!" I shouted, struggling to break free, but when I turned to look at Nathan I couldn't believe my eyes! He was just standing there watching! And there were no claws trying to grab him at all! I was holding onto the cylinder for dear life while being pulled by the vicious zombie!

Chapter Seven - Scary

I couldn't stop fighting now! I managed to sit up while I was being pulled towards the opening. I lifted the cylinder and rammed it into the zombie arms clutching me.

CRACK! The arms smashed to smithereens, and I broke free!

I stood up and smashed the arm that was grabbing onto Sissy, using all my might to crush it! Sissy fell to her knees, holding her neck.

"You ok?" I asked.

"I think so…" she choked, but there was no time to spare. Arms and claws kept breaking through.

Nathan had sat down next to us now with his flashlight, and I couldn't help but notice that a few of his fingernails had turned completely black. He must have banged them at some point.

"Look! This tunnel goes on, let's move!" I whispered. We crawled further in – it looked like a smaller, strange passageway. It was a long, hard crawl, as I had to push the cylinder ahead of me.

I didn't feel as positive as I did before. This time I wasn't so sure we were going to get out of this place alive. Maybe it was because Nathan was acting so odd, or maybe it was the fact that we were now battling two types of Lizenbog – dead ones and live ones. And the Nougous were nowhere to be seen. *Had they just deserted us? Little did I know that soon I would have my answer.*

It felt like we were crawling for days. Sissy was first, I was second and Nathan was behind me. It was a relief to get away from the zombies again, but I couldn't help but fear what would happen around the next turn. Every once in awhile I could swear I heard hissing. It must've just been my imagination.

Finally, we came to a hole at the end of the passageway, all the more thrilling because it was lit by a small glimmer of light. We were finally getting out of the darkness!

"Look Sissy! Look Nathan! Light!" I cried.

We moved quicker to get out of the tunnel, and when we came to the end Sissy and I inched our way out of the narrow opening into some other strange part of the cave.

It was different from the rest of the cave. It looked almost like huge square boulders lining the walls. There was no other way in or out besides where we had just come from – except for the small opening, about fifty feet up on the ceiling, where the light was coming through. However, it would be impossible to get up there, and even if we could, we would never fit through the hole.

"How weird, it looks like someone has been here before," I said. "There's no way that those square boulders were formed that way."

We stood up on wobbly legs and brushed off our knees and hands, which were scraped from crawling. It felt great to stretch out our legs – until I noticed that Nathan had still not come out.

"Where's Nathan?" Sissy asked.

"I was just wondering that myself!" I answered.

"Nathan?" I said, picking up my flashlight and bending over to look back into the long, dark tunnel. The minute I did I knew the nagging feeling I had all along about Nathan was true! But it was worse than I ever could have imagined! Nothing could have ever prepared me for the terror that happened next!

Chapter Eight - Scary

Hhhhhhhiiiiissssss!

I jumped a mile! I couldn't believe my eyes when a huge Lizenbog came flying out of the tunnel that we just crawled out of! But it wasn't a zombie Lizenbog! And it wasn't a living Lizenbog!

"It's Nathan!" I gasped as shivers went up and down my spine. I knew we were doomed! I grabbed Sissy and we backed away as it's repulsive face – hissing and drooling a disgusting orange slime – lunged right up into mine.

"Nathan! Mick what are you saying? Have you lost your mind?" Sissy screamed, until she noticed that this grotesque creature had Nathan's clothes on!

"Oh nooooo! You're right!" Sissy cried. "How could this have happened?"

"The cut! The cut on his back!" I replied as we backed away. My stomach turned just looking at him!

Nathan had completely transformed. He had huge spikes pointing out of his back, and he had turned completely green with long black alien Lizenbog claws on his hands and feet.

He was lurching right at us, ready to tear us apart!

“Run Sissy! Run the other way!” I yelled. We ran in different directions. Nathan turned his head quickly back and forth both ways, not knowing who to go after first. I was hoping he would chase me, but he went straight for Sissy. He took one huge jump and knocked her to the ground! I stopped dead in my tracks. I had to do something, so I tried to distract him.

“Nathan! Nathan! Here I am! It’s the cylinder you want isn’t it?” I taunted him.

He pinned Sissy to the ground, lifted his huge Lizard head, and turned my way. Orange slime poured out of his mouth.

"That a boy! Over here! You don't want some silly girl now, do you?" I teased.

I thought for a split second that I had his attention and he would move my way. A disgusting snarl curled over his dreadful fangs and then he started to go right to Sissy's face! My blood ran cold and my heart sank! He was going to devour Sissy!

"Nathan, please stop! Your hurting me!" I heard Sissy say as she started to cry.

I couldn't just stand there and watch this happen! I grabbed the cylinder, which had fallen to the ground in all the confusion, and threw it right at Nathan. I didn't want to hurt him, I just wanted to save Sissy.

The cylinder missed him. Now he was furious! He jumped up with reptilian fast moves, grabbed Sissy with his right arm, and within seconds, he had a hold of me with his left!

"Ouch! I screamed as his black razor-sharp claws dug into my skin.

"Nathan, don't do this! Stop! Come to your senses!"

He started swinging us around like rag dolls. Then he pushed us both to the ground and clutched us under the sharp talons on his feet! I stared straight into his eyes, trying to find a hint of Nathan, but there was nothing there – just pitch black evil eyes and a blood-thirsty Lizenbog alien!

Chapter Nine - Scary

Nathan's grasp suddenly loosened when an explosion of blue light suddenly filled the room! It was radiating through the hole in the top of this mysterious place and was so bright we squinted! It was the Lizenbog blue scanning beams!

I felt totally defeated!

But instantly realized that maybe we still had a chance! Nathan was so distracted that he let go of Sissy and me. I motioned for her to roll away if Nathan moved. He did! He moved toward the light! *We were free from his brutal grasp!* Sissy and I rolled to a far wall.

"I have a plan!" I whispered.

"Yeah, I hope it's a good one," Sissy answered, rubbing the deep red indents Nathan's ferocious claws left on her arms. "cuz I am a bit freaked out here…and to even think that I laughed at the thought of aliens!"

That instant the blue beam grew even brighter.

"Darn it!" I blurted out.

"What?" Sissy asked.

"The blue beam! It's locked onto the cylinder…

it's the living alien Lizenbog! Let's try to get back to the tunnel!"

We carefully scooted back to the passageway that we had crawled from. Nathan was distracted, watching the cylinder slowly lifting by the blue beam. Small rocks fell from the top of the cave. More and more bright light filled the room as the hole in the ceiling grew wider and wider!

Now we could see sharp black Lizenbog claws digging and chipping away at the ceiling. If I could get Sissy safely in the tunnel, I might be able to make one last effort at grabbing the cylinder.

But as soon as we got to the opening, "Agggggghhhhh!" We both screamed. A stomach-turning skeleton arm reached out for us!

The zombies had found us! *Now There were Lizenbog pouring in from everywhere, live Lizenbog from outside and dead zombies through the passageway!* We threw ourselves against the wall of the cave and huddled in fear, watching the most ghastly sight you could ever imagine.

Both groups of Lizenbog filled the room. While the cylinder remained suspended in mid-air they began slithering around it in circles, staring at each other. The hissing sound in the room was overwhelming! I was horror struck because now I knew that it was the end of the world!

Chapter Ten - Scary

I couldn't believe what happened next! Instead of joining together, they began snarling at each other. The Lizenbog's tongues snapped at the zombies, who in turn clawed at the air, as if they were ready to rip them apart. Slowly they circled around the cylinder. They were each just inches away from it.

"What's happening?" Sissy asked.

"I don't know! It looks like they aren't on the same team," I replied.

"Team? What do you mean *team?* I really don't consider this a sporting event!" Sissy whispered sternly. I was happy to hear that she had a bit of her sassiness back.

"OK, so not on the same side –whatever," I answered. And I was right! The living Lizenbog grabbed the cylinder, but the second he did the zombie grabbed it too! Instantly it became a tug-o-war!

"OK, now it's a sport!" Sissy said, sounding somewhat relieved considering the situation that we were in, but I was relieved too! *They were not on the same side!*

The tug-o-war had turned into a battle, and the cylinder tumbled to the ground as they fought, clawed, and punched each other. Lizenbog were flying everywhere. Sissy and I were stuck on the sides of the room and had to keep moving to avoid being hit, and we were covered in orange slime and the sand that shook out of the zombie Lizenbogs bones.

I kept my eye on Nathan, who was straight across from us, watching everything. In all of the commotion and fighting he had completely forgotten about the cylinder, and so had the rest of them! I got on my knees and started to crawl in to grab it.

"Oh no you don't!" Sissy said, grabbing my arm and stopping me. "Look!" She pointed to the opening at the top of the cave. Nougous were flying in with jetpacks! We were going to be saved! But our happiness vanished seconds later.

Chapter Eleven – Scary

I quickly remembered that without the cylinder in their hands the Nougous didn't have the strength to fight off the Lizenbog, let alone zombies! I was going to have to get that cylinder!

"Sissy, let go! They won't be able to save us without the cylinder!" I whispered.

"Then I'm going with you!" she snapped back.

At this point I didn't have time to argue so I replied, "Alright already! But whatever you do, don't scream."

We crawled in and around the fighting, while dead Lizenbog and zombie pieces were flying everywhere. We crawled over them and under them, trying to get to the cylinder. I glanced up at the Nougous – they seemed to know what we were doing while they hovered above the room.

Luckily, nobody had noticed them. When we were just feet away from the cylinder, Nathan jumped right in front of us, hissing and clawing!

"Back up Sissy! Slowly!" I whispered. We started to crawl backwards, but Nathan grabbed my shirt and pulled me face-to-face with him!

"Let go of him!" Sissy scolded, slapping Nathan's nasty claw right off my shirt.

Nathan did a double take at Sissy, just as a Nougou landed right on top of the cylinder behind him! Nathan turned and hissed at the Nougou. But the minute the Nougou touched the cylinder a glowing purple force field lit up. Immediately the Nougou pushed the glowing buttons on his metallic cuff and at once, a test tube like cylinder encapsulated Nathan. Seconds later, it completely folded into a thin line and vanished!

"Nathan!" I screamed. The Nougou looked at me and nodded as if to say that he would be alright. In all the chaos we hadn't noticed that the fighting had stopped and the Lizenbog were slithering our way!

Two more Nougous touched down on the cylinder and linked hands. The purple force field immediately covered them. They quickly leaned forward and touched us, and we were instantly encased in the strange magnetic field!

Lizenbog – dead and alive – tried to grab us, but the power of the electrical field fried their claws right off! They were angrier than ever! Some of them were so mad that they threw themselves right at the force field – which caused them to burst into flames. Sparks and orange goo were flying everywhere, and the zombies simply crumbled to dust.

The Nougous ignited their jetpacks and we lifted to the ceiling. I couldn't believe that we were really getting out of this horrible cave!

Chapter Twelve – Scary

We were heading straight up and out, right towards the awesome blue sky! We couldn't look back again! We had the cylinder and we had been rescued, but I couldn't help but think about Nathan. What if they couldn't help him and he would remain a Lizenbog forever?

Once outside, we landed on top of the cave. Other Nougous were waiting to lift the cylinder directly to their ship, the Stal-ite, which suddenly became visible and was right above us.

More Nougous descended from the mothership. They formed a circle around the hole in the top of the cave and hit their cuff buttons in unison. Streams of glowing hot light filled the cave. A swirling sea of what looked like hot lava filled the room below us, completely covering the Lizenbog. The horrible hissing stopped.

Four more Nougous came down from the ship with the negotiator. We were so glad to see him we jumped up and down and he did too, but the ceiling of the cave started to sink. It was going to collapse! Instantly we were lifted by the Nougous up to the ship!

As we looked back, we watched the dreadful cave implode upon itself. We were escorted into the ship with the negotiator.

"You have done a phenomenal thing Mick Morris," he said.

"Hey, what about me! Am I like invisible or what?" Sissy exclaimed.

"You as well, girl-kind," the negotiator answered.

"See he doesn't know my name but he knows yours…" Sissy expressed her disapproval to me, but she had no sooner done so when suddenly a huge smile came over her face!

"Nathan!" she screamed, running toward a giant glass test tube that was slowly being drained of a gray jelly like substance. As it drained, we watched Nathan slowly turn from a hideous lizard alien back into himself. His eyes were wide open, and he stood frozen, looking at us in disbelief. Once he was fully human the capsule pulled up into a compartment and Nathan stiffly stepped out.

"Whew! That was weird!" exclaimed Nathan. "I knew what was happening the whole time but there was nothing that I could do. I was completely taken over!"

"Well thank goodness you're OK, dude!" I said as we high-fived.

The negotiator interrupted. "We must get the cylinder back into its proper place on planet Nougou. We would like to stay and practice earth-like emotions, but we must return to our galaxy."

"No problem, I think we better get back too!" I replied.

"We cannot thank you enough," the negotiator said.

"Thank you for saving us! Call it even!" I replied.

'We will now guide you back to your area," he said, while other Nougous strapped us into jetpacks.

As we were guided out of the ship, we were flown over the smoldering, rubble of the cave. I glanced down at it and felt a total wave of fear. I wasn't quite sure why – probably just the ordeal that we had gone through. We were safe now, and so was the universe!

I thought so anyway. Little did I know that on the floor of the smoldering cave one black, ferocious, zombie Lizenbog claw was scratching at the sand.

The End?

CHAPTER ONE - SUPERHERO

Just then something totally weird started to happen. The cylinder, which had been shiny silver, took on an eerie green glow. I was freaking out, too, because ever since we entered the cave the cylinder felt like it was shaking. It was such a small quiver that I wasn't sure if it was because I had been running, or if something else was happening to it.

"Hey Sissy! Nathan! I know this sounds weird, but I think this cylinder is starting to shake," I said.

"Maybe it's because were running – but we gotta keep moving!" Nathan said.

I could tell that he was really terrified, but trying to hide it. *He wasn't the only one!*

When I looked toward the outside of the cave my stomach did flips. "Look!" I screamed.

The Lizenbog pods were landing right outside the cave!

"Oh no! There's no way we're going to be Lizenbog leftovers! Let's go!" I yelled.

The huge, threatening, black Lizenbog ship was right behind the pods, coming up over the ridge. We didn't have a second longer to talk. Nathan and Sissy grabbed the backpacks as I lifted the cylinder to my shoulder and once again we ran as fast as we possibly could. We were running deeper and deeper into the huge, scary, black cave.

The further in we got, the more the cylinder shook – but even weirder, it was starting to make a "*Hhhhmmm – Hhhhmmm*" sound.

"What's up with that thing?" Nathan asked.

"I don't know, but it's getting worse," I said.

"It's glowing like a giant light stick!" Sissy cried.

She was right, it was glowing so brightly that its light filled up the entire cave.

"Well, at least we can see," I replied. "Besides, maybe there's a reason this thing is freaking out. I get the feeling that may be part of the Nougous plan."

The cylinder began shaking harder and harder as we kept moving. It was shaking so violently that I wanted to stop and put it down. My arms were feeling really funny, like I was resting them on one of those vibrating chairs.

I was ahead of Sissy and Nathan, and it felt like the cylinder was guiding us. As I ran, I carefully slid the cylinder down off my shoulder and tried to carry it in front of me. The harder it shook, the brighter it got! It was as if it was helping me decide which twisting, turning path in the cave to take.

We were dodging streams and rock formations as we followed the strange twists and turns. I was sweating so much that it was hard to hold onto the cylinder. But I knew that it was leading us somewhere.

I just hoped the Lizenbog didn't get us first! As we ran, we could hear noises echoing through the cave – footsteps, hissing, growling, and falling rocks bouncing off the walls throughout the catacombs behind us. The fast, slimy Lizenbog were gaining on us! They would catch up to us in seconds!

CHAPTER TWO - SUPERHERO

Sissy was getting really tired and starting to slow down.

"Sissy, you have to keep moving! Can't you hear them getting closer?" I said, panting while I ran.

"But Mick, how are we gonna find our way out of here? Or how do you know that we won't be trapped by them deep in this cave?" Sissy replied. "Mick, did you hear me? How are we…?"

"Don't worry, Sissy! I know we're on to something, but we have to be quiet and keep moving!" I said.

The cylinder's shaking became unbearable. My arms were numb, and the hum was growing louder with every turn. The louder the hum became, the louder the Lizenbog hissed! They were gaining on us, and I couldn't hold onto the cylinder anymore! *I tried to hold it but suddenly it slipped right out of my hands!*

"Oh no!" I screamed.

I stopped abruptly. Sissy and Nathan ran right into me. We were shocked as our faces lit up from the neon green glow of the cylinder, because instead of hitting the ground...*it levitated! There it was, just floating in mid-air*!

"What is going on?" Nathan asked, his eyes growing huge as he stared at the cylinder.

"This is creeping me out!" Sissy said, barely able to get the words out.

Bright green light filled the cave. Then, the cylinder started to move through the air – all by itself!

"C'mon, we gotta stay with it!" I yelled over the loud hum.

We followed the cylinder, running faster and faster just to keep up with it. Left, then right – it was like running through a maze! The hum was getting louder, to the point of hurting our ears. We could no longer hear our footsteps, nor the hissing of the Lizenbog – nothing but the hum of the cylinder.

Then without warning, the humming just stopped, and so did the cylinder. Then it slowly started to move again. We kept a few feet behind, following and watching closely.

It finally stopped right in front of what looked like a round room made completely out of rock. It was so weird, it almost looked like someone had purposely carved out this dome-shaped room. The rocks were smooth.

The cylinder moved into the room and we carefully followed. We were terrified now, but there was no turning back. Then I saw it! On the inside of this strange room, the familiar hieroglyphics, the same writing as the Nougous had on their ship! They did this! *They had been here before!*

CHAPTER THREE - SUPERHERO

The bright, neon green cylinder glided to the middle of the room, as if it knew where it was going. The eerie glow changed to focus towards the top and bottom of the cave. It looked like some kind of laser beam going in a straight line from ceiling to floor, with the cylinder hovering right in the middle of the beam.

Then it began to change, within seconds the cylinder looked like it was starting to melt. It was! The silver metal was turning into a liquid! Drops of shiny silver liquid fell to the floor, but even weirder, drops were going up to the ceiling, then disappearing!

PLOINK! PLOINK! *It sounded like coins dropping to the floor and hitting the ceiling at the same time!* The three of us watched in amazement. As the metal melted away, I could see that there was something underneath it.

"Nathan, what is that?" I whispered.

"A naturally occurring inorganic solid with a chemical composition..." he began to answer.

"English Nathan! English, please!" I snapped.

"Oh right, sorry. It looks like some sort of crystal," Nathan answered.

That was it! Now we could see it, under all of that silver metal was a glowing green crystal. The beam intensified as the last drop of metal dripped away. It looked like a huge, green, emerald, the size of a large water bottle. It was still suspended in the center of the room by the brightest beam of light that I've ever seen.

Unexpectedly a weird feeling of energy filled the room, pulsing through us.

"Mick! Mick, what is happening here? What's going on?" Sissy asked.

I tried to answer, but I couldn't. Within seconds our bodies began to ripple like waves, and there was nothing we could do about it!

I could see Sissy next to me. She looked like she was on a carnival ride! Her fists were clenched while her body did the wave. Her neat hair stood on end, just like mine – it looked like we were in some sort of weird electrical storm. I wanted to see Nathan, who was next to Sissy, but I couldn't lean forward. I tried, but *an unexplainable force was moving my body*. What happened next changed us forever!

CHAPTER FOUR – SUPERHERO

There was a blinding explosion, a sudden flash of green, then a huge bright white light that was so powerful it knocked us to the floor! I tried to focus, but couldn't. I felt totally weird, like I was looking through green night vision goggles. I felt a weird sensation all through my body.

When I finally had the strength to get up and could focus my eyes, I crawled over to Sissy and Nathan. Nathan was brushing off dust, coughing, and starting to sit up. Sissy was sitting with her legs crossed, rubbing her eyes. I stood up, and helped Sissy get up.

"Are you guys okay?" I asked.

"Yeah…I think so," Sissy answered.

"Yeah, oddly enough, I feel pretty good," Nathan said, smiling and pounding his chest, which was so unlike him.

The crystal was no longer floating in midair – it was lying in the middle of the floor. It wasn't glowing anymore either, and the mysterious beam was gone too. Then I realized that I could see, but what was weird about that was that the cave had no light source in it, *anywhere.*

"Hey, guys, I have a question. How are we able to see right now?" I asked.

"Huh?" Sissy said.

"Think about it. The cylinder is gone and the crystal isn't glowing. There's no way we should be able to see," I said, blinking my eyes open and shut.

"So what if we can see, what just happened is just way too weird…" Sissy said.

"Sissy," Nathan interrupted. "We don't even have flashlights! We're seeing in the dark!"

"Maybe it's because of the green flash," she said. "Yeah, that flash might have…"

Sissy's words were cut short by the Lizenbog claw that suddenly grabbed her shoulder. She gasped, frozen with fear, just staring at us.

One of the Lizenbog had snuck in behind us while we were trying to figure out what had happened. The Lizenbogs ferocious claw dug into her right shoulder. Another vicious claw grabbed her left arm. It peered it's ugly, scaly face over her head, hissed at us, and began to pull Sissy out of the strange rock room!

The hissing sound grew louder and filled the room as other Lizenbogs slithered in toward us!

"Sissy! Run!" I screamed. "Run!"

She instantly snapped out of her shock and tried to move, but she couldn't break the Lizenbogs powerful, sharp grasp. When she turned to face the Lizenbog, it quickly grabbed each side of her head! Its claws covered the top of her head, its large mouth opened and hissed at her. Long, razor-sharp teeth were right next to her face, as the Lizenbog lifted her off the ground. This was it! Sissy was caught in its deadly grasp! *The Lizenbog was going to eat Sissy!*

CHAPTER FIVE – SUPERHERO

Just then, Sissy did something I couldn't believe! She screamed! Now, I've heard her scream before, and according to her mom, she does it often. But not like this! She let out the loudest, most high-pitched, ear-piecing scream I've ever heard in my entire life! It sounded like an eagle's call, but a hundred times sharper and louder! Even more startling was that it didn't stop! Her scream was so powerful the cave began to shake and rocks were falling everywhere!

"EEEEEEeeeeeeoooooaaaaaaahhhhhh!" Sissy screamed.

Nathan and I covered our ears, but for some reason it really didn't bother us. *But what it did to the Lizenbogs was unbelievable!*

They screeched in pain, and dropped to their knees. They tried to cover their tiny ear holes, but it didn't help. The horrible Lizenbog that had Sissy in its evil grasp was launched across the room and hit the rock wall – BAM! PLUNK! – and fell to the ground!

They had all been blasted by Sissy's incredible shriek. When she stopped screaming, we stood there in disbelief. Lizenbog were scattered all over the ground, knocked out!

"That was fun," Sissy said, fixing her hair.

“Oh, man! Can you believe that?” Nathan asked, looking at me. “If she does that all the time, then no wonder she gets on your nerves!”

“Uh…?” I said in disbelief. “Sissy, what…uh…how did you do that?”

“I don’t know…I just opened my mouth like this…” she replied, starting to open her mouth wide again.

“No, no, no! We heard you the first time,” I answered.

“So did they!” Nathan said, pointing at the Lizenbog bodies scattered all over the ground.

We noticed that a few of the creature’s claws were beginning to move.

“They’re coming out of it!” I said. “We have to get out of here, now!”

Sissy had the strangest smile on her face as we hurried out of the bizarre cave room, climbing over the Lizenbog bodies. Once we were outside of the rock room we started to run again, until I realized that we had forgot something

“Wait! We have to go back and get the crystal,” I said.

“Why?” Nathan asked. “Why do we have to go back there? Mick, you know those creepy alien lizards are starting to wake up! They’re not going to be happy about what ‘Miss Sissy-Screamer’ did back there. In fact, I bet they’re really mad!”

"Take it easy Nate," I said. "You know that the crystal holds the key to keeping our planet and the entire universe safe! Everything seems to have happened in this cave for a reason. Maybe we had to bring it here."

"Hey! I can just scream at them again!" Sissy said proudly.

"Can you…I mean…do you think you can do that again?" Nathan asked.

"I don't know. I guess so. Actually, I'm not sure. I've never done that before," Sissy answered.

"Well, what if you can't? And those Lizenbog are waking up and…" Nathan was interrupted when a bat slammed into his back.

"LIZENBOG!" he screamed. But what happened next was truly unbelievable! *Nathan disappeared!*

CHAPTER SIX – SUPERHERO

All I could see was the small cave bat flutter away – and Nathan was gone!

"What happened? Oh my gosh! What happened to Nathan?" Sissy cried.

I could see dirt shuffling, and shoe prints moving in the same spot where Nathan had been standing!

"Nathan? Nathan, buddy where are you?" I yelled.

"I'm right here! Darn, that bat scared me!" Nathan replied.

Sissy and I jumped.

"Right where? We can't see you!" I exclaimed.

"Very funny Mick!" snapped Nathan. "What did I tell you about cracking jokes when things aren't funny?"

"Nathan I'm not kidding!" I said.

There was silence for a second then Nathan slowly said, "Oh man…how cool! I'm invisible. This is unreal! Check me out. Well, you can't, but hey…"

Suddenly Nathan appeared before us!

"We can see you!" Sissy said.

"Oh man, totally awesome! I can turn it on and off by just thinking about it. Watch!" Nathan said excitedly.

He appeared and disappeared three times in a row. Nathan had the power of invisibility! Something weird was going on! But it didn't matter now, because Nathan's new invisibility was just what we needed to get the crystal back!

The Lizenbog were struggling to wake up when Nathan entered the round cave room. He carefully tip-toed around the horrible creatures, while Sissy and I waited around the corner. Sissy bent down in front of me just in case she had to do her screaming thing again.

The Lizenbog leader that had attacked Sissy was the first one to get up on its feet. It still looked groggy as it shook its head back and forth. Spit flew out of its mouth as it tried to hiss out a command in its native tongue. The others were slowly moving too. We could see by the shifting sand on the ground that Nathan was making his way to the center of the room. The Lizenbog leader was up and moving! As it stumbled towards Nathan, it stopped and sniffed the air, sensing something. Its ugly face looked to the right, then quickly to the left, then it stared right at Nathan. Without even knowing it, it was only inches away from Nathan's face! Then something caught its evil orange eye.

"I think it can see him…or smell him, or something…I better get ready," Sissy whispered.

The creature was looking at the ground – it had spotted the crystal! Something that seemed to resemble a smile curled up over its sharp teeth. As it reached for the giant gem, WHAM! It instantly flew backwards, and again it hit the cave wall with a huge THUMP!

Nathan had hit him as hard as he could, right under the jaw. He remembered what an uppercut punch was and the Lizenbog leader would never forget it!

The crystal disappeared the instant Nathan picked it up, and we could see by the cave floor that he was making his way towards us. The Lizenbog knew something was going on and they were furious! They were jumping up with their sharp claws ready. They saw the footprints and started chasing after them! *They were onto us and we were doomed!*

CHAPTER SEVEN – SUPERHERO

"Sissy! Sissy!" Nathan shouted. "As soon as I pass by, do your thing!"

A Lizenbog swiped at the air in the direction where Nathan's voice was coming from, then hissed wildly.

"Now!" Nathan screamed, as his footprints ran past us. Sissy stepped forward, directly in front of the mob of Lizenbog.

"EEEEEeeeeeeyyyyyaaaahhh" Sissy bravely screamed, harder and louder than before. The sound blast sent the Lizenbog flying backwards one on top of the other, squirming again in pain. Rocks fell from the ceiling near the room entrance, completely covering them. Suddenly the entire rock room began collapsing. We ran out backwards! The room completely crumbled crushing all the Lizenbog inside! They were finished!

"Whooo hooo! Take that, you repulsive reptiles!" Sissy shouted.

"Way to go Sissy!" I yelled. Then I realized that Nathan was still invisible.

"Where's Nathan?" I asked.

"Here I am! Wow! That was pretty weird," Nathan said, magically appearing before our eyes. He handed me the crystal, which I put in my backpack.

"Yeah, something strange is happening, but we still have to get out of here," I said, as we hurried toward the cave entrance.

I was beginning to wonder what was really going on with Sissy and Nathan. Nathan could now turn invisible at will, and Sissy could scream out a sound loud enough to knock aliens to the ground in pain. That green blast must've had something to do with it. They both had some sort of superpower. Something had changed. And I was glad it did, because now nothing was going to stop us from saving the planet! But I couldn't help but wonder why I didn't get any superpowers. I still felt the same, maybe they were just in the right place. My thoughts quickly changed when we turned a corner, and I could see what was waiting for us right outside of the cave.

"Stop!" I whispered. "Lizenbog!"

"Oh no! Not again," Sissy said. "How many this time?"

"Wait here behind this rock, I'll go check," Nathan said.

In a blink, Nathan turned invisible, and within seconds he was back.

"Okay," he said. "There's easily two hundred or more Lizenbog. Mick, we can't go out this way."

"I don't think we have a choice. These catacombs all lead into that round room, there's no other way." I said.

"Let me at them!" Sissy said.

"Do you think that you even have a scream left in you?" I asked. "I'm talking about a scream to end all screams?"

"I think so," Sissy replied. "But then what?"

"Well, we'll think of something…" I replied.

"Think of something – I know!" Nathan said. But he said it just a bit too loudly.

The Lizenbog heard him and were making their way towards the cave. Our luck had run out, this was it! *We were now going to be Lizards Lunch!*

CHAPTER EIGHT – SUPERHERO

"EEEEEEeeeeaaaaaahhhhhoooouuuuuuu…" Sissy's first screech knocked several Lizenbog backwards out of the cave, BAM! FOOOMMP! They went flying!

Nathan and I were right behind Sissy but he was invisible. The entrance was clear! *But, as soon as the first wave of Lizenbog tumbled backwards, more came forward!*

Sissy would run at them screeching and blasting them backwards, but every time she did more Lizenbog would run at us! There were just too many of them!

Sissy's voice was getting tired – every scream was a little bit shorter. When we finally had a clearing, we ran out of the cave and away from their pods and ship! Sissy was ahead of me, and by the moving footprints in the sand, I could see that Nathan was right behind her. Just as I got a few steps away from the cave I felt giant lizard claws sink into my shoulders! The Lizenbog had caught me! We didn't see the Lizenbog sitting on the side of the hill waiting to pounce on us!

Before I knew it, they were leaping at me from all angles! I could feel the sting of their long, scaly lizard tails wrapping around my legs. They attacked from the right and from the left – there were too many of them for Nathan or Sissy to save me!

"Run! Run, save yourselves!" I tried to scream when I felt a jagged Lizenbog claw cover my mouth.

Now that made me mad. It made me real mad, in fact it mad me SUPER mad! I was so angry I couldn't contain myself! I decided it was time to teach these lizards a lesson!

I felt my whole body tighten up – it felt like my muscles were exploding out of my body! I began to twist, turn, and roll. I could hear the hissing as the Lizenbog began to fall off of me. CRUNCH!!! SMASH!!! SPLAT!!!

When I had almost broken free, I started picking off the remaining few one-by-one – as if they were tiny fleas – and tossing them back into the cave. KABANG! POW!

CRUNCH! They kept coming, and I kept knocking them out!

Some of them tried to escape, but that's when I heard Sissy.

"EEEEEeeeaaaaaoooouuuugggg!"

She was screaming at the top of her powerful lungs.

Now I could stand up, and I continued slapping and kicking the lizards into the cave with a simple flick of my wrist or foot when they tried to attack. FLINK! PLUNK! WHAM!

Before I knew it one of them had managed to get on my back and tried to wrap its huge, scaly tail around my neck! I was choking – I couldn't breathe! I tried to get him off of me, but I was getting light-headed…I was losing my power…I felt myself beginning to pass out.

CHAPTER NINE – SUPERHERO

"SSSSssssssssssssss…" the Lizenbog around my neck started hissing.

Just as everything started to go black I felt the Lizenbog tail around my neck loosen. It was being pulled off of my neck! I could breathe again!

"A little help here," I heard Nathan say.

"Thanks Nathan," I hoarsely whispered, grabbing the tail the invisible Nathan was desperately trying to get off of me. I held onto the tail tightly and began to spin this last menacing Lizenbog above my head in mid-air.

"Here you go, you slimy alien – this is the last of you!" I shouted. "Duck, Nathan! Duck, Sissy! This Lizenbogs going for a ride!" I sent it sailing down the ravine.

"Way to go, dude!" I said to Nathan as he became visible. "You saved my life!"

"No kidding!" Sissy exclaimed. "And Mick, when did you get so strong?"

"I don't know! I just couldn't take it anymore and something happened," I replied. "I guess that I did get some of my own superhero powers!"

"Well, that was awesome!" Nathan said. "We did it! We saved the universe!"

"The universe – yeah!" I said. "Wait a minute – the universe! The crystal! We have to get it back to the Nougous! Where's my backpack? We have to find it!" I exclaimed. "It must've popped off when I gained my super strength!"

We looked everywhere.

"Found it!" Sissy yelled from behind a boulder, holding the backpack in the air.

"Let's go!" Nathan said.

Just then huge gusts of dust blasted from under the Lizenbog ship as the engines roared. The huge, black, Lizenbog ship began to lift.

"One sec…" I yelled. "Just one last thing I need to do!"

I ran and jumped as high as I could, landing on top of the Lizenbog ship just as it began to slowly lift off. It was low on power, and I felt like I was on a surfboard. I knelt down, and with both of my fists I began to pound on the ship as hard as I could. It was a struggle – I would pound, and it would go back down, then power up and rise again. I was done with this game and these horrible creatures as I lifted my enormous fists over my head then came down with all of my might. This time the Lizenbog ship hit the ground. I jumped off, picked it up over my head and heaved it down the ravine. It looked like a shiny, black wheel rolling and bouncing down the side of the hill. When it hit the bottom, it exploded into a giant fireball!

"There! Now I feel better," I said.

Sissy walked over and handed me my backpack.

"Awesome job. Mick!" she exclaimed.

"That was *sweet!"* Nathan said.

We began to find our way down the hill. Suddenly, another huge, black shadow lifted over us.

Oh no! I didn't think that our super powers would hold out for another battle with those awful aliens! This was it! Game over!

CHAPTER TEN – SUPERHERO

Nathan went invisible, Sissy opened her mouth – ready to scream – and I clenched my fists. As the ship began to come over the ridge, our biggest fears were put to rest! It was the Nougous!

We backed away from the ship as the enormous ramp lowered to the ground. The Nougougian negotiator and their leader came down the ramp, followed by the other Nougous.

The Nougou leader spoke, and the negotiator translated: "You have saved the planet, our life form, and the universe. For this we will be forever thankful."

"Your welcome," I replied. "And we will be forever thankful that you helped us save Sissy."

"Me too!" Sissy smiled.

"Yep, all of us!" Nathan added.

I took the emerald green crystal out of my backpack. The Nougougian leader motioned behind him, and two Nougous ran up, carrying another large silver cylinder. They opened it up, and the leader placed the crystal in it, immediately it filled in to the exact sized compartment.

"It fits perfectly," I exclaimed.

The leader spoke and the negotiator said, "Just like you and your new powers."

Sissy, Nathan and I looked at each other.

"We will now take you back to your people," the negotiator said.

"Well, if you don't mind, could you just drop us off nearby?" I said. "They are…well they just might not…well let's just say that they are kind of busy."

"Kind of busy. Earth kind are busy. I get it," the negotiator replied.

"Yeah! You got it!" I laughed, and the negotiator laughed with me.

We climbed into their ship and within seconds were strapped in and talking off, then landing. We said our good-bye's and waved to the Nougous. We started walking up the hill towards the set, but something was missing! Nathan!

"Very funny Nathan!" I said, as he popped back into sight. We all had a good laugh.

I guess sometimes you never know what you could be myth-ing!

THE END

Chapter One-Short

I was exhausted, and there was a piercing ringing in my brain! It sounded almost like a siren.

"EEEEAAAHHH – EEEEAAAHHH – EEEAAAHHH!" This awful sound, over and over again, and getting louder! Even though the sand was almost soft and comfortable, I figured this must be how the Lizenbog destroy their enemies – by painfully breaking their eardrums!

I didn't know how I was going to stop it! The next thing I knew there was a glimmer of light shining in my eyes. There must be another way to escape! The light was growing brighter and brighter!

I looked up and saw that it was the sun coming in! Only it wasn't coming through a hole in the cave – it was coming in from my bedroom blinds, and the "EEEEAAAHHH – EEEEAAAHHH!" sound was my alarm clock!

"What? What?" I said, shaking my head to snap out of it.

It had all been a dream – or maybe a nightmare, depending on how you look at it. But even worse than that, I knew that it was starting all over again when I heard:

"Miiiiccckk…Mick are you ready? We're leaving in five minutes!"

"I'll be right down, Mom!" I yelled.

The End

Glossary

Abduction-To take someone away against his or her will, kidnapping.

Action-A command called by the director, which means to begin acting and filming.

Ad lib-Unrehearsed, unscripted action or speech, unplanned.

Alien-a being from another planet; sometimes used to describe a stranger or foreigner

Audio-Relates to sound, speaking, music, sound effects.

Background-Areas appearing behind the main focus; can also pertain to background music or sound effects.

Blast-off-A rocket or spacecraft that is takes-off is launched.

Boom-An elevated support system for cameras or microphones that suspends the object and can move it up, down, or sideways during filming.

Cast-Performers in the play, movie, and television show etc.

Close-up- A tight shot of the subject that is being filmed or photographed.

Cut-A command used by the director on the set, which means to stop all action.

Director- The person who is in charge of all matters on the set of the show, the filming, the cast and the crew.

Edit-The final stages of cutting the film together in the studio by picking shots, adding sound and openings and credits.

Extraterrestrial-From another planet, said to be a being from outer space.

Flying Saucer-Any mysterious round shaped flying object; supposedly piloted by aliens.

Focus-Adjusting the lens to achieve a sharp image.

Live-The camera or microphone being on while the show is being filmed, or a live show is a show that is telecast while it is happening, not pre-recorded.

Location-A specific place where the show or movie is to be filmed.

Props-Articles used to decorate the set or to perform with.

Remote-A production that is filmed away from the studio-on location.

Scene-The location where the action is being filmed or a grouping of shots.

Script-The actual detailed description of the program or movie; which includes dialogue, direction, and technical instructions.

Set-The actual room, or place on the location where the show or movie will be filmed.

Shooting-The actual rolling of the film during the taping of the show.

Special Effects-Illusions created either in front of the camera or added later electronically.

Talent-The actors that appear in the show.

UFO-Unidentified Flying Object-A mysterious object in the sky that cannot be explained, said to be vehicles carrying extra-terrestrials.

Voice Over-The words heard by the audience by someone who is off camera.

Witness-A person who has actually seen something happen.

Wrap-To end the shooting and begin packing up.

Zoom-To either "zoom-in" having the picture get closer on a subject or "zoom-out" showing more in the frame.

About the Breges

Author Karen Bell-Brege just so happens to be married to the illustrator, Darrin M. Brege. *Mick Morris Myth Solver* is their second book together, following *The Chill Art Sketchbook.*

Karen is a comic and public speaker. Darrin is also a comic, and has created tons of illustrations for national companies, and all of the original covers for the *Michigan and American Chillers* series.

The Brege's have one son – whose name, as if it is any surprise – is Mick! They all live in a funky old townhouse in the Midwest, and their favorite thing in the world to do is laugh. On rainy nights, they have a blast making up crazy, fun, scary stories.

MICK AND THE GANG ARE OFF TO OREGON FOR ANOTHER EXCITING ADVENTURE. VISIT WWW.MICKMORRIS.NET TO FIND OUT WHEN THE EXCITING SEQUEL WILL BE IN STORES!

Contact us and visit
www.MickMorris.Net
for...
New Book Info
Signings and Visits
Drawings
Photos
and more!
DON'T CATCH THE CHICKENS!
Play the
CATCH A MYTH GAME
only at
WWW.MICKMORRIS.NET